Fallen Angel

HEATHER TERRELL

Fallen Angel

HARPER TEEN

An Imprint of HarperCollinsPublishers

HarperTeen is an imprint of HarperCollins Publishers.

Fallen Angel
Copyright © 2011 by Heather Terrell
www.harperteen.com

Library of Congress Cataloging-in-Publication Data
Terrell, Heather.
    Fallen angel / Heather Terrell. — 1st ed.
        p.   cm.
    Summary: When sixteen-year-old Ellie meets up with a boy from
her past, she discovers that the two of them share inexplicable powers
and that they are somehow involved in an ancient conflict among fallen
angels that forces them to choose sides, with terrible repercussions.
    ISBN 978-0-06-196570-8
    [1. Supernatural—Fiction. 2. Angels—Fiction. 3. Good and
evil—Fiction. 4. Interpersonal relations—Fiction. 5. High schools—
Fiction. 6. Schools—Fiction.] I. Title.
PZ7.T274Fal   2011   2010013688
[Fic]—dc22   CIP
                                                                  AC

Typography by Tom Forget
11 12 13 14 15 LP/BV 10 9 8 7 6 5 4 3 2 1
❖
First Edition

For Jim, Jack, and Ben

"How art thou fallen . . ."
Isaiah 14:12

Prologue

I watched my curtains billow in the early autumn wind that wafted through my opened bedroom window. The night beckoned to me. And I answered its call.

Lifting the bedcovers off me, I walked over to the window and floated out into the darkness of midnight. The wind surged behind me, as I flew through the shadowy streets of my town. Weaving between the familiar shingled homes of my sleeping neighbors, I reveled in the sheer pleasure of flight and the secrecy of my journey.

I was so lost in the sensation that the tall steeple of my town's eighteenth-century church loomed before me unexpectedly. The church's spidery, whitewashed spire stopped my progress, momentarily forcing me to drop and hover in midair in front of the church's circular stained glass window. Although the window was colorless in the night sky, I swear it stared at me like a preacher from the pulpit. Judging me. Why had I never noticed the window before? In my other dreams?

Without warning, the wind picked up speed and whipped at my face. It was cool and damp, and smelled of the sea. Suddenly, the church and the town structures and even the streets felt confining, and I longed for the openness of the ocean.

My shoulder blades lifted and expanded. I streamlined my limbs to gain speed. Taking a sharp left away from the church, I headed toward the bracing—and freeing—air of the nearby sea.

Civilization disappeared as I raced along the jagged cliffs and rocky beaches of the Maine coast. The ebb and flow of the great ocean waves crashing on the shore below began to lure me farther and farther out to sea.

A bright flash on a rocky promontory caught my attention. The light burned brightly—and inexplicably—in the deep darkness of the moonless night. Tearing myself away from the hypnotic enticement of the tide, I swooped down to the promontory to inspect this unanticipated deviation in my recurrent dream.

As I neared the stony outcropping, I saw that the light on its surface wasn't a fire or a lamp. It was a man. What looked like a light was the shimmer of his blond hair, so white it gleamed even in the scant illumination of the night.

The figure stared out at the sea, hands in his jeans

pockets. He looked young, maybe around my age of six-teen. I flew a little closer, but not too close. I wanted to see him, but didn't want to be seen.

Although his face was hazy in the dim light, I felt a pow-erful connection to him. An attraction. He had green eyes and surprisingly suntanned skin. With such pale hair, I expected that he'd be fair.

He adjusted his position, and I could better see his almond-shaped eyes and cleft chin. But the more I stud-ied his face, the more it changed. The eyes looked blue instead of green. The nose lengthened just a touch, and the lips filled out. He no longer looked young like me, or old like my parents, but sort of ageless. His features became more perfect and angular, and his skin grew paler and paler, almost as if his human flesh was turning to smooth, cold marble. Nearly as if a master sculptor had fashioned a human being into an ethereal creature.

Then he turned and stared at me, as if he knew I'd been there all along. And he smiled a horrible, knowing smile. His perfect face no longer seemed the sculpture of an angel but a demon, and I knew I looked into the face of evil itself.

I opened my mouth to scream in terror. And then I fell.

ONE

I fell to earth with a thud. Or so I thought.

I opened my eyes and saw my bedroom. I was lying on my tall sleigh bed, with the weak sun of early morning starting to stream through my blinds. The dream had been so real that I half-expected to find myself sprawled out on the promontory instead of back at home under my warm covers.

Still, the dream clung. Rubbing my eyes to wipe it away, I heard a familiar voice call up the stairs.

"Ellie."

I still felt kind of drugged by the dream. I moved my lips to answer but couldn't get out much more than a croak.

"Ellspeth? It's time to get up."

The spell of the dream lifted the moment my mom's voice got louder and she used my full name. She only called me Ellspeth—my old-fashioned given name, which she knew I hated—when she was really irritated with me. My voice returned, and I responded to my mom. "I'll be down in a minute!"

Disentangling myself from my sheets, I slid off the bed and padded over to my dresser, where I'd laid out my clothes for the day. I shivered; I could actually see my breath in the air. Why was it so cold?

I looked around the room and saw that my window was ajar. Just a crack, but enough to let in the chilliness of the Maine autumn morning. I didn't remember opening it before I went to bed. Odd, but I could be a bit absent-minded at times.

I closed the window, gathered up my clothes, and headed down the short hallway to my bathroom. Shutting the door behind me, I turned on the water—hot. Then I lathered lemony soap onto a damp washcloth, and took my first look into the mirror.

I ignored the pale, almost translucent, blue eyes looking back at me as best I could: their odd, unsettling color had brought me nothing but stares for years. Instead, I focused on the things I could control. I studied my face, wondering for the millionth time just how I'd tame my unruly, obstinately straight black hair. Picking up my brush, I began the long, painful process of undoing all the knots, yawned, and slowly awakened to the sunny morning.

Its brightness drove away the creepy ending to my dream

and lifted my spirits a tiny bit. I thought maybe I'd be able to make it through my first day at the upper high school after all. Then again, I'd probably still wish I could fast-forward through all the nonsense—past the hallways and classrooms full of social posing and gossipy distractions from schoolwork—and go straight to college.

Within the hour, I was careening through the hall-ways crowded with all-too-familiar seniors and juniors. I approached my newly assigned locker with a single, silent prayer on my lips: "please, please, for once let Piper's locker not be near mine." In an unfortunate twist of fate, I was regularly subjected to the uber-popular Piper Faires both at home—where she was my next-door neighbor—and at school. Our last names—Faires and Faneuil—doomed me forever to be Piper's locker neighbor as well. The fact that Piper routinely ignored me at school, while still acting like my friend at home, made the whole situation very awk-ward. Although I had to admit, our unavoidable in-school proximity and neighborhood friendship had benefits: they brought me a certain immunity from her group's petty little games.

Scanning the lockers, I didn't have to look too hard or too long before I spotted my assigned number twenty-four, and realized my prayer hadn't been answered. There stood Piper with her swarm of friends circling around their queen—Missy—like honeybees. With their even tans, perfectly faded jeans, and colorful summer flip-flops, they glowed and seemed carefree—even young—in a way I'd never experienced. With all our environment-saving missions to impoverished countries, my parents had imbued me with such a strong sense of responsibility to the world at large that I never really felt happy-go-lucky. If I ever had a minute to spare, I felt like I should be volunteering more hours at the local soup kitchen instead of just hanging out.

I knew I shouldn't care about their little pack, and really, truly didn't care most of the time. After all, Piper had "invited" me to be part of her inner circle back in middle school, and I rejected her. Even then, I just couldn't stomach being part of a group that routinely voted their friends "off" the lunch table, relegating them to some "loser-ridden backwater table" until they were voted back "on." Still, in such close proximity to their light, I couldn't help but feel like a black hole, with my dark hair and jeans.

Missy, the most malevolent of the group, leaned directly on locker number twenty-four. My eyes rolled at the thought of having to cut through all Missy's nastiness to get to my locker before the bell rang. She caught my gesture, and I braced myself for some sort of backlash. Instead, Missy flipped her golden brown hair over her shoulders and said, "Hey, how was your summer?" With a smile.

I turned to look behind me, wondering just who she was talking to. My relationship with Piper ensured that Missy never bothered to belittle me, but she sure never bothered to be nice, either.

She repeated herself. "How was your summer, Ellie?"

"Fine," I answered warily, as I opened my locker. I busied myself inside it, slowly organizing my books in the hopes that she'd disappear by the time I emerged.

It didn't work.

"Where'd you go this time?" Missy asked when I peeked out.

"Kenya," I said as I shut my locker. That she admitted to knowing my name and the fact that I took summer trips abroad was beyond me.

"You're so lucky your parents take you all over the world. I was stuck here in Tillinghast all summer long."

I didn't know what to say to her, especially since Piper and the rest of the golden group were watching with expectant grins on their faces. And especially since I was pretty sure that Missy's glamorous vision of my world travels didn't jibe with the third-world reality. So I didn't say anything.

Missy filled in the silence. "The girls and I were just talking about meeting at noon for lunch. Want to join us?"

I was just about to ask why when Ruth walked down the hall toward me.

Ruth's pace slowed and her shoulders tensed when she spotted me talking to Missy. Ruth knew that she'd have to pass by her to get to me, and that the immunity my relationship with Piper bought me didn't extend to her, even though she was my best friend.

I watched as Ruth bravely squared her shoulders, tucked her long red hair behind her ears, and approached me. Compared to the suntanned perfection of Missy and her friends, Ruth looked plain with her pale skin, wire-rimmed glasses, and basic T-shirt and jeans. But I knew that she hid a quiet prettiness behind that camouflage; it was just that she hated any kind of attention, even the positive variety.

"I think the bell's about to ring, Ellie," she said. Our first class was AP English, and rumor had it that the tough Miss Taunton was a stickler for timeliness.

Before I could respond, Missy swatted her hand in the air. She said to her little audience, "Did you guys hear something?"

The other girls snickered. I shot a quick look at the uncharacteristically quiet Piper. I didn't expect Piper to defend Ruth, but I was happy to see that she didn't chime in.

"No?" Egged on by her friends' laughter, Missy batted the air and continued with her little charade. "Must be some nasty fly."

"What did you just say to Ruth?" I said, unable to keep the anger from my voice, which only made me really mad at myself. Missy's clique delighted in belittling those who could not—or would not—wear the "right" skinny jeans or date the "right" senior jocks. The bigger the reaction, the better. I didn't like to satisfy them—or feed their little games—with any sort of reaction. Particularly since Ruth was plenty capable of defending herself in the classroom and in the hallways, if she so chose. And today, she did not so choose.

Missy waved her hand around again, and this time, it nearly brushed up against Ruth's cheek.

I felt anger sweep over me like a wave, something I'd promised my peace-loving mom to avoid ever since I got into a nasty argument this summer with a spiteful member of our mission. I sensed my fair skin turning a fiery red and experienced the oddest sensation of my shoulder blades lifting and expanding.

Without thinking, I grabbed Missy's wrist. Suddenly, the school hallway faded away, and I got a vivid flash of six-year-old girl Missy as if I were her. She stood at the edge of the pool at the posh Tillinghast country club she so often bragged about. In the image, a group of boys and girls teased her about her buck teeth and knock-knees. Missy turned around, looking for the protection and consolation of her mother. Her mother was indeed watching. But rather than answer the call for help in her daughter's eyes, she gripped her gin and tonic and walked over to her own gaggle of friends, many of whose children were teasing Missy. Her mother kept pretending she'd never seen the weakness in Missy's eyes. In that very moment, the young Missy promised herself to never show that weakness again. She vowed instead to create that weakness in others, to make others buckle at her feet.

I started to get another, more recent, image. Missy was locked in a tight embrace with a guy. Looking through Missy's eyes, I couldn't see the guy's face, but I could hear his low, gravelly voice whispering in her ear. At first, I couldn't make out his words, but I could feel the warm, feathery sensation send shivers down Missy's spine. Then the words became more distinct, and I swear he said, "Ellie." But the guy could only know my name from Missy, and why would she bother to talk about me?

Lost in that thought, I was jarred back to reality by Ruth, who was trying to pull my hand off Missy and whispering, "C'mon, Ellie, she's not worth the bother." The image disappeared as quickly as it came, bringing me back

to the horrible, and very real, teenage Missy. Yet, of the
two images, the childhood scene remained so real to me
that I felt Missy's six-year-old feelings and thought her six-
year-old thoughts as if I were the six-year-old Missy, and I
experienced a deep sense of pity for her.

It wasn't the first time I'd had this kind of flash, as
I'd come to think of them. They'd been occurring more
often since my sixteenth birthday in June, although they
usually didn't amount to much. Usually, they showed me
what people had for lunch or told me what they thought
of their friends' outfits. In the beginning, I thought my
imagination was just going into overdrive, but it wasn't
long before I realized that what I was hearing and seeing
in my mind wasn't made up. It was true. One of the first
times it happened, I imagined the girl sitting behind me
in Spanish class was wondering about whether to break
up with her boyfriend, and then a few seconds later she
turned to her friend sitting next to her and asked about
that very thing. But who could I tell without getting
locked up for delusions?

Despite Ruth's attempt to pull me away, my grip on
Missy's wrist tightened as my feelings about her swung
wildly between sympathy and rage. She didn't move; I
guess she was too stunned by my action to lash out with
one of her usual barbs or even yank her hand away. We

stood frozen until I felt Ruth's hand forcibly pry my fingers off Missy's wrist and lead me away.

"What were you thinking, Ellie? You know I can take care of myself with those idiots," Ruth whispered as she pulled me toward our classroom. I could tell she was mostly mad that I'd put myself in jeopardy; Ruth was very protective of me.

"I'm sorry, Ruth, I know you can. I really don't know what came over me," I whispered back.

We grew silent as we wove slowly through the crowded hallway. I felt someone staring at me, and I turned, hoping that it wasn't Missy or her crew behind us ready to retaliate.

It wasn't. A tall, impossibly blond-haired guy was leaning against a door frame, watching me. He smiled a wry smile as though he'd seen the whole scene with Missy and company, even though he couldn't possibly have witnessed it from his vantage point. He wasn't traditionally good-looking, but he seemed older than the average high school guy. His body language was comfortable in a way that I'd never seen before in the other guys. I usually hated arrogance. But this was something else. He had an easy confidence that I was surprised to find instantly attractive. I felt certain that I didn't know him—an oddity in the town where I grew up and where

I recognized pretty much everyone.

The bell rang. "Oh my God, we can't be late on the first day with Miss Taunton," Ruth said and picked up the pace. I let her drag me away from his penetrating gaze. And away from my own pounding heart.

Two

I forgot all about him over the next week of school. That was the little lie I told myself as I embarked on advanced English, history, chemistry, Spanish, and calculus, all of which had piled on their workload this year, supposedly to prepare us for college.

But the truth was, I was distracted. I looked for him everywhere. The relative smallness of the upper school—just a hundred students for the junior and senior grades—made his absence that much odder. It was almost like he was a figment of my imagination.

But I couldn't really ask Ruth if she had seen him too. I'd never hear the end of it. For years I'd been proclaiming indifference and immunity to guys our age. I'd never really felt comfortable with them. They always seemed silly or self-important, and I never felt like I had any common ground with them. Or they with me.

But by lunch on Friday, I was scanning the tables and

the cafeteria line for this guy. I could hear the buzz of voices around me, but my focus was elsewhere. It didn't help that I was exhausted. My nightly dreams were getting more and more vivid, and I woke up feeling as if I'd been up all night. The details would get fuzzier as the day went on, but every night I'd be back in the sky, flying over the town.

"Ellie, are you listening to me?"

I turned to Ruth. "Sorry, what did you say?"

"I swear, you're like a ghost these past few days. Where are you?"

I thought about how to answer that loaded question. Should I tell her about Missy and company's suspicious continued attempts at friendliness and blame my distractedness on that? I knew that Ruth didn't really care that much about their clique, but no one liked to be snubbed and they weren't exactly seeking her out, even though Ruth and I were kind of a package deal. Or should I stick with the overwhelming schoolwork as the excuse for my preoccupation? I sure didn't want to pin it on some mystery guy in the hallway. "I'm sorry, I guess the teachers' constant harping about college has got me distracted. What were you saying?"

"I was actually talking about colleges. Geez, you really are somewhere else, aren't you? There wasn't some guy in

Kenya this summer that you've been keeping to yourself, was there?"

Ruth's suggestion was ridiculous given the stark reality of my summer in Kenya, and I almost laughed. Until I saw her face. She looked really hurt at the thought that I might keep something from her. I would have thought that my best friend of seven years—almost like the sister I didn't have—would know better.

But Ruth was complicated. Anyone close to her could see that she was witty, smart, dependable, and intensely loyal, albeit the kind of loyal that occasionally bordered on possessiveness. But you had to get close to see all her wonderful qualities, which wasn't easy. Ruth lost her mother to cancer when she was in first grade—only months before we met—and she was afraid to let people in, in case they left her, like her mom. To protect herself, she'd erected enormous barriers to friendship, and I was one of the only ones who'd managed to surmount those walls.

"No, I swear. I was up to my elbows in composting and African animal manure. It was hardly a glamorous atmosphere to meet a guy."

Ruth laughed. "Gross. But knowing your parents, I'm not surprised." Satisfied, she started talking about her wish list of colleges and the criteria for acceptance, who got in at what rates and all that stuff. I wished that Ruth didn't worry so much; I knew she'd have her pick when the time came, even though she'd have to rely on scholarships and financial aid to pay her way. Her dad's salary as a grounds-keeper at the university didn't go too far.

We bussed our trays and made plans to meet up at the coffee shop after school. I walked back to my locker to switch out my English textbooks for Spanish, hoping to avoid Missy and her friends if at all possible. Letting out a sigh of relief as I neared number twenty-four without Piper's trademark auburn ponytail in sight, I saw him— standing by my locker.

He couldn't be waiting there for me. It had to be a coinci-dence. Whatever his reason, I sure wished that I'd stopped in the bathroom after lunch and at least brushed my hair.

Up close, he was better-looking than I remembered, even though he was more striking than cute. But his eyes, so pale and green, unsettled me. Much as mine must unnerve people, I suddenly realized. It was the first time I'd seen anything like them on another person.

I almost couldn't talk as I reached my locker. But I didn't have to. Within seconds, he said, "You look different."

I reminded myself that I'd never met this guy before. What did he mean, and who did he think he was, talking to me with such familiarity? "Different from what? I don't know how I could possibly look 'different,' when we've never met before," I said and buried myself in my locker.

"We have. Three summers ago. In Guatemala."

That stopped me short. I had been in Guatemala then. As I took my time sorting through my books, I racked my brain. Three summers ago, I had tagged along with my parents' university training program to a remote, rural area in Guatemala. My parents were college professors specializing in organic farming and, during the summers, they organized trips to destinations around the world, teaching local farmers' methods to increase production in an earth-friendly manner. Not exactly the jet-setting world travel that Missy probably envisioned. I was expected to roll up my sleeves just like all the other professors, students, and local farmers, so I got to know everyone in the summer programs really well. But I had no recollection of this guy. And he was the kind of guy you'd remember.

This had to be some kind of prank. Maybe this was Missy's backup humiliation plan because her attempts at faux friendship were failing. Why else would a cute, new senior be approaching me, claiming some nonexistent past acquaintance? Not that I thought I was without charm, mind you, but I was hardly the typical pick for a good-looking senior.

I would not be made a fool, especially by the jerks who thought of themselves as popular. As if that label meant anything in the scheme of life.

Slamming my locker door shut, I said, "I don't know what you're talking about."

As I started to walk away, I heard him say, "You don't remember the University of Maine agricultural outreach program in Guatemala? Three summers ago? We were both there with our parents."

The confusion in his voice sounded real. And so did his command of the details. No way Missy would have known all that. No way Piper would have remembered it from our few neighborly conversations. I turned around. He actually looked hurt.

I was about to risk further discussion, when Riley—one of the most popular senior guys and a star athlete—walked by and grabbed his arm. If this guy was friends with Riley, I definitely wasn't his type. Assuming this wasn't a joke, of course.

Before I could say anything, Riley started to drag him down the hallway. "Come on, Chase. We'll be late for practice."

THREE

"Do you remember a guy named Chase? From one of our summer trips?" I asked as casually as possible over dinner that night. I kept my eyes down and played with the pasta on my plate to avoid contact with my parents' perceptive eyes. I wasn't used to being coy with them; I'd never had anything of interest to hide. But saying the question aloud made me feel oddly exposed.

"Chase?" my mom asked.

I didn't look up from my plate, but I swore I heard something like alarm in my mom's usually serene voice. Normally, she was irritatingly unflappable, the tougher of the two. And infuriatingly beautiful, by the way, despite an avowed aversion to makeup or anything that resembled "fashion." Only in the past two years had a few lines appeared on her totally natural face and a few grays in her chocolaty-colored hair. Of all their peers and friends, only my dad rivaled her in looks; it was annoying having such attractive parents.

"Yeah, Chase."

"That doesn't sound familiar," she said.

My dad piped in, almost too casually. "I don't remember a 'Chase' either. Why do you ask?"

"Because he introduced himself to me at school today. He's new. He said he remembered me from the Guatemala trip."

Out of the corner of my eye, I saw my dad shoot a look at my mom. "Now that I think of it, the name does ring a bell. Chase, you said?"

"Yes."

"Huh, I seem to recall a nice-looking couple and their son. I think the parents were ethnobiologists. Chase is their last name, if I'm not mistaken."

I groaned. "Now I really feel like an idiot."

"What do you mean?"

"When this Chase guy came up to me, I drew a complete blank."

"Well, it was three years ago, and that team was unusually big. In fact, it was one of our biggest and busiest projects, so I'm not surprised that you don't remember him," my mom quickly interjected.

"Your mom's right, Ellie," my dad said as he got up from the table and started clearing plates.

"It's just really strange that I have no memory of him at all, especially since there usually aren't any kids my age on the trips. Do you remember his first name?" I asked.

"Michael, I think," my dad answered. He cleared his throat and turned on the water in the sink. "Did this Michael—if that's even the right name—say why his family moved to Tillinghast?"

"We didn't get that far in the conversation. I felt embarrassed about not knowing who he was, even though he claimed we'd met, so I was a little rude. Really rude, actually." I groaned again. "I feel awful now."

"Don't worry about it, dearest. You can always apologize."

"True." I stood up and began helping my dad with the dishes. As I handed him a rinsed plate for loading, my fingers brushed up against his arm, and it occurred to me that—for all the flashes I got when I touched people—I never got one when I touched my parents. But my thoughts quickly returned to Michael. "To answer your question, I bet his parents are working at the university. I mean, where else would they be working in Tillinghast as ethnobiologists?" Although Tillinghast used to have a bustling millinery industry back in the eighteen hundreds, it was now sort of a one-horse town in terms of employment. Nearly everyone served the university in some capacity or other—whether as professors or as store-owners or something in between.

"But I don't think I saw their names on the roster of visiting professors. Did you see any Chases on the list, Hannah?" he asked my mom.

"No, Daniel, I didn't." She answered quietly, staying seated instead of getting up to help us clean the kitchen as she usually did.

Why was she acting so strange? I wondered. Was it really that weird that I'd asked about a boy? I kind of wished I'd never brought it up. Then again, maybe my parents were just being their normal awkward selves; they always seemed to be acting the role of parents, uncertainly searching around for the right line. I always chalked it up to their being academics through and through—not really entirely in this world.

"Oh, well, you're probably right, Ellie. I'm sure the university brought them here. We'll probably run into Michael's parents in the halls before long," my dad said.

"I'm sure we'll run into the whole family soon enough," my mom echoed, finally rising from the table. "It's a small town, after all."

As I continued to rinse off plates and pass them to my dad, I cringed inwardly thinking about my exchange with Michael. On one hand, I felt relieved that his claims to know me weren't a hoax, but on the other, I knew I'd have to apologize next week.

The phone rang. My dad picked it up and made some small talk before handing it to me. "It's Ruth, dearest."

Before I could even say hello, Ruth launched in. "Where were you? I called your cell, I texted you—nothing. I finally just went home. Not cool, Ellie."

"What do you mean?" I was genuinely mystified.

"The Daily Grind? After school?"

In my haze over Michael, I had forgotten about our plans to meet at the coffee shop. I wandered into the family room, so my parents couldn't overhear our conversation. "Oh Ruth, I'm so sorry. It totally slipped my mind. Can you forgive me?" I felt terrible. Ruth's early experience losing her mother made her worry about people's welfare, among other things.

"Of course. Don't be ridiculous. But you had me worried. You never forget things. What's going on with you?"

"Can I chalk it up to jet lag? We got back less than a week ago." I scrambled for an explanation, any explanation.

"Yes, but please promise to keep your cell on. Okay?"

It annoyed Ruth to no end that I routinely failed to turn on my phone. No one ever called me on it except Ruth and, in emergencies, my parents. "I promise."

"Now, you're not going to forget our plans to go to the

movies tomorrow night, are you?"

I laughed in relief at the mock scolding in Ruth's voice. "Of course not. Would I miss Audrey Tatou's latest?" We both adored foreign movies, though for very different reasons, and went nearly every weekend. Ruth loved how different cultures told stories, while I was drawn to the exotic settings. Ruth could never understand why I didn't get my fill of that over the summers. No amount of explaining on my part could make her understand that farming in rural Kenya or Guatemala bore absolutely no resemblance to the Parisian café culture.

"Good. I'll see you at seven at the Odeon."

FOUR

On Monday, I expected to pass Michael in the hallways and get the cold shoulder, at best. In fact, I wouldn't have been surprised if he told me off for my rudeness; he would've been justified. I certainly didn't anticipate— or deserve—seeing Michael waiting for me with a friendly smile on his face. But there he was.

Michael stood against the wall near my locker so casually that, once again, I thought maybe he wasn't waiting there for me. After all, he could have any number of reasons for being there. But then he waved and smiled at me. A fierce blush spread across my pale cheeks when I realized he was waiting for me. How did he know where my locker was?

Although I shyly returned his smile and wave, I got more anxious as I walked toward him. Michael wore average-looking jeans and a black T-shirt, but he looked different—more mature, maybe—than the average Tilling-hast guy. Plus, I had this business of apologizing to address.

Michael's warm smile made the apology a lot easier. I bit the bullet and said, "Hey, I feel really bad about not recog-nizing you at first on Friday—"

He interrupted me. "Don't mention it. It's been three years, and we both look different. You especially," he said with an appreciative glance that made me blush. I hated to blush. He seemed to notice my discomfort, and rushed to lighten the mood by teasing me. "I hope I look different than I did three years ago, too. Maybe better?"

I laughed a little, but didn't know what to say next. I never knew what to say to guys, unless it was about class work or organic farming. Obviously neither topic lent itself to casual banter, although normally I didn't mind. And anyway, I still had this weird amnesia when it came to Michael and Guatemala, and I didn't know how to avoid that topic in a conversation since it was our main common ground.

We stood in what seemed, to me, like an eternal awk-ward silence. To fill the void, I started walking down the hall, and he quickly followed. But the quiet finally got to me, and I blurted out, "So, your parents want to save the world, too?" I figured that he could relate if his parents dragged him on far-flung missions to Guatemala, like mine did.

"Something like that," he said pleasantly enough. Maybe I had passed the first conversational hurdle. "We've traveled all over for their work, that's for sure."

"Did your family move here so your parents could teach at the university, M—?" I almost said his name, and then I stopped myself. Technically, we hadn't introduced ourselves, and I definitely didn't want to admit that I'd discussed him with my parents, and got his name that way.

"We moved to Tillinghast over the summer so my parents could work on a special project."

"So it's just a temporary move?" Even though I barely knew this guy, I felt disappointed that he might not be in town for long.

"We're here until the project meets its goal, I guess."

Before I could ask any other number of polite, conversational questions, he turned to me with a broad smile and asked, "So where are we headed?"

"English."

"What are you reading?"

"*Pride and Prejudice.*"

"I had to read that for English last year. I thought my teacher would never stop talking about it. I think she's still looking for her Mr. Darcy."

I had to laugh. I had heard the same thing about my English teacher, Miss Taunton.

We started talking about *Pride and Prejudice*, which I'd read on the long, hot Kenyan nights when there wasn't much else to do. In fact, I had finished the assigned *Pride and Prejudice* and worked my way through all of Jane Austen over the summer. He asked me what I'd thought of the novel. I loved it, and he admitted that he'd found it slower than molasses and about as interesting. But he said it with the kind of smile that made me forgive him for having such a negative view on a book that I loved. I'd never had this kind of conversation with any other guy before. With anyone other than Ruth, actually. My parents and their colleagues stuck to practical scientific texts and world issues, and my other friendships were of the superficial variety. And even though we didn't agree, it was such a rush to find a guy that I could talk to—after so long pretending to myself and everyone else that I didn't much care that I couldn't speak the language of guys my own age.

Too soon, we stood near the entrance to my English class. I paused near the door. I felt awkward about how to break off. Would it be really 1950s of me to thank him for walking me to class?

"Well, it was really nice seeing you again. . . ." I let

the sentence drift off as I faced the uncertain business of whether I should say his name or not. I hoped he didn't notice.

He did, of course.

"Michael. Michael Chase," he interjected and then smiled that disarming smile again. "In case you forgot."

"Right, right. Thanks, Michael. And I'm—"

"I know who you are. You're Ellie Faneuil."

He started down the hallway toward his own class, but then turned back suddenly with a devilish grin. "Actually, you're *Ellspeth* Faneuil, aren't you?" With a wave, he walked away.

FIVE

To my surprise, Michael sought me out each day that week. I'd step out of class, and he'd be waiting nearby. I'd pop out of lunch and head to my locker, and he'd be strolling alongside me down the hallway. His constant attendance never seemed weird. In fact, his easy manner and our effortless conversations—mostly about classes—made it feel really natural. By Friday afternoon, my reserve about him had chipped away.

Just before two o'clock, I stood in the back of gym, waiting for Ruth to join me before I sat down for the principal's first assembly of the school year. The space was crowded with bleachers and chairs, instead of the usual sports equipment. Students were beginning to pour in.

I spied Missy and her usual entourage approaching my spot, and I just didn't want to interact with them. So I slid away into a darkened corner next to the bleachers. From there, I could still see the doors to the gym and catch Ruth's attention when she arrived, but didn't have to deal with any of Missy's annoying, ongoing efforts at friendship.

As I watched the clock tick closer to two and the seats fill, I wondered where Ruth was. Ever punctual and organized, it wasn't like her to be late. Not to something like this. I didn't dare take one of the few remaining chairs without her; she'd be furious at having to sit alone.

Ruth. Just thinking about her reminded me that I hadn't mentioned Michael. Our somewhat conflicting schedules meant that she hadn't seen me with him. And I hadn't felt like telling her about our conversations yet. I just didn't want to bump up against that overprotectiveness of hers when I wasn't even sure that there was anything between Michael and me for Ruth to protect.

The clock hit two, and the principal strode across the stage. Craning my neck, I scanned the room to be certain that I hadn't missed Ruth. The gym was packed with students, but no Ruth. I settled back into my little nook and waited. I would give her one more minute before I snagged one of the few open seats nearby. At this point, she'd have to understand.

Without warning, I felt a presence in my dark alcove. I hadn't seen anyone approach my little corner, so I was confused by the sensation. I looked around. But there was no one standing to my left or right.

Then I felt a hand on the small of my back. The light pressure sent chills up my spine, and my heart started racing. I did not need to turn around to see who it was. Somehow I knew it was Michael behind me.

Removing his hand away from my back, he inched closer. "Is this spot taken?" he whispered, as he sidled up next to me.

We'd never been so close to each other. I felt like I could hardly breathe, let alone answer. Where had this strong, physical attraction to him come from? Over the past few days, I'd grown to really like him, but I hadn't experienced anything like this with him. Or anyone else, for that matter.

"No," I finally managed, with a gulp.

"Good. Maybe I'll just stay here with you instead of sitting down, if that's okay. That way, we can scoot out early."

"Sure," I answered with what I prayed was a calm voice. Even though I felt anything but calm.

The lights dimmed, making our dark alcove even darker. The principal began to rustle some papers on the podium. He tapped the microphone, which let out an ear-piercing shriek. Michael and I turned to each other, covered our ears, and laughed. Then we stood next to each other in companionable silence while the principal started his speech.

I heard Principal Robbins greet the incoming class of

juniors and welcome back the seniors, but I wasn't really listening. I heard the crowd laugh politely at some lame joke the principal told, and I smiled along with them as if I were paying attention. But all I could hear and see and feel was Michael.

Principal Robbins introduced the vice principal, and quiet fell over the crowd while he walked across the stage to the podium. In that brief silence, Michael leaned toward me. I could feel his warm breath on my cheek, and I wondered what he was going to do or say.

He nudged me in the direction of the gym doors and said, "I think someone's looking for you."

I looked over. In the darkness of the gym, a person stood silhouetted against the bright light streaming in from the opened doors. It was Ruth.

More than anything in the world, I wanted to stay alone in that alcove with Michael. But I knew I couldn't. I had to signal to my friend.

Before I motioned for Ruth's attention, I turned back to thank Michael for pointing her out. But he was already leaving.

As he walked away, I thought I heard him say, "Maybe I'll see you this weekend."

Six

The weekend that followed was long and filled with misgivings. Michael never reached out to "see me" like I thought he had said. So I had way too much time on my hands to stare at my neglected cell phone and think about him.

I couldn't help but wonder why Michael had been so persistent in seeking me out over the preceding week. Not that he'd declared a specific interest or anything, but he clearly went out of his way to see me during the school days—for friendship or more I couldn't quite tell. Could it really be that we had connected on that Guatemala trip? And why me? He seemed to have made other friends in the short time he'd been in Tillinghast, the sort of guys who hung out with the most popular girls and ignored the rest of us. I couldn't help but feel like Michael would start ignoring me, too, one day.

By Monday morning, I had my guard back up. So when I stepped out of English and spotted him talking to a group of jocks instead of waiting alone for me, it seemed that my fears were confirmed. Fears that he'd given up on our tenuous relationship, fears that he hadn't been genuinely interested from the start. I let my hair hang in front of my face, and walked in the opposite direction to avoid passing him. Even though it was the wrong way to my next class.

Darting down the hallway as quickly as I dared, I heard my name being called out.

"Ellie."

I knew it was Michael's voice, but I was so embarrassed that he might have caught my glance and my hasty exit that I kept moving.

"Ellie." His voice was getting louder, and I could hear his footsteps approach. But I kept pretending I couldn't hear him.

Michael reached my side, and reached out for my arm. It tingled where he touched it. "Ellspeth," he whispered, and his breath sent shivers up my spine. The long, disappointing weekend had done nothing to change his physical effect on me.

I stopped walking and turned to look at him. He seemed upset.

"I know you saw me. Why did you walk away?"

"You seemed"—I reached for an explanation—"busy. I didn't want to interrupt."

"You should know that I'm not interested in them. I'm interested in you."

"Really?"

"Really."

Our eyes locked for a brief second, when I realized that Piper and Missy were walking nearby. And watching our every move.

Michael must have realized it too, because he broke my gaze and changed the subject.

"Sorry I didn't get a chance to call you this weekend. Did you have a good one?" he asked as we started walking down the hall again.

"Yeah, I guess so." I desperately wanted to ask what kept him from calling, but I didn't want him to think I'd fixated on his parting words from Friday.

"How'd you like the movie on Saturday?"

"You were at the Odeon?" I was shocked. No self-respecting Tillinghast upper-class guy would be caught dead at the Odeon, which only showed foreign movies and independent films. From what I remember, the theater was almost empty.

At the mere mention of the Odeon, Piper and Missy giggled and walked away. In that split second, they clearly decided that Michael—no matter how cute and how senior—wasn't worth their attention. He had revealed himself as an indie-movie-watching geek. I was relieved.

Michael answered as if totally unaware of, or even better, uninterested in, the judgment just passed by Missy and
crew. "I came in late by myself. You and your friend looked
like you were having so much fun that I didn't want to
interrupt you guys."

"You were there by yourself?" I blurted out and then my
cheeks flushed. Of course I wanted to know if he'd brought
a date, but why did I have to be so obvious?

He smiled. "Yeah, I was. That's probably not very cool,
is it? To go to the movies on a Saturday night without any
friends?" But he didn't seem the least embarrassed. In fact,
his ability to do whatever he wanted without worrying
about the social consequences was one of the things I liked
most about him.

If possible, I got even redder. I hadn't meant to insult
him, but at least he didn't grasp the real reason I'd asked
the question. Or at least he had the decency to pretend that
he didn't.

Michael continued, "I've lived in enough places that I've
learned not to care what is cool. I've learned to suit myself.
And anyway, Tillinghast is a small place. It helps to get out
of it for a while, even if it's just at the movies. If that makes
any sense at all."

"It does." He made it sound acceptable, rather than

strange, to spend a Saturday night at the Odeon. And I really did get what he said. Having spent so much time in other cultures, I shared his compulsion to escape from the confines of Tillinghast into other worlds.

He changed the subject back to the movie, a French film. Before long, we were back on track and engrossed in a discussion over the best French movies. I favored the Three Colors Trilogy, while he advocated for *La Femme Nikita* with its stylized action scenes.

We arrived at my calculus class door too quickly. For me, anyway. The embarrassing moment of departure arrived once again. But before I could say anything silly, Michael said, "I wanted to ask you—"

"Ellie, there you are!" Ruth bounded over and landed directly between us. "You almost forgot this in my car this morning, and you ran out of English before I could hand this to you." She stuck out a folder and handed it to me. I took the folder from her, careful not to touch her directly. Since the flashes started, I always took extra care to make sure I didn't get any from Ruth. Late last school year, I accidentally brushed up against her arm as she was looking at Jamie, a junior guy she often described as "thick," and I saw that she actually had some pretty intense feelings for him. I didn't want any more flashes from Ruth. It would make our friendship really weird.

I stared down at the folder Ruth had jammed into my hand and realized that it contained my calculus homework. "Oh, wow, thanks, Ruth. I can't believe I almost left it behind."

Looking up, I saw that Ruth was gaping at Michael— and speechless. I realized that Ruth had leaped between Michael and me without realizing that we were talking. Why would she think that I'd be talking to him? After all, I'd made a conscious decision not to mention him to her. But based on her reaction, it was clearly a very bad decision. I definitely wished that I had brought up Michael already.

What else could I do at that moment but introduce them and try to act normally? "I don't think you two have met. Ruth Hall, this is Michael Chase. Michael, this is Ruth."

"Nice to meet you, Ruth," Michael said.

Still Ruth said nothing, just kept staring. You'd think she'd never seen a guy speak to her best friend before.

Since he was getting no response from Ruth, Michael turned back to me and continued where he left off. "Anyway, Ellie, I know it's early in the week, but I wanted to ask if you were free this Saturday night. Maybe we could go to the Odeon together?"

I shot a glance at Ruth, whose mouth had literally dropped open. We had talked about going to see the new Odeon release ourselves, this upcoming Saturday night.

"Actually, Ruth and I had plans—"

With a start, Ruth came out of her spell. "Ellie, I forgot to tell you that I have a family party to go to on Saturday night. So you're free, you're totally free."

Family party? Ruth didn't have any family besides her dad. That was one reason she'd gotten so close to me and my parents, and her dad had gotten so tight with my mom and dad. That, and the fact that her dad and my parents shared a near-obsession with the environment. Ruth was really looking out for me, despite the shock at seeing me talk to Michael.

"Great," Michael said with a smile at Ruth. He looked at me again. "Should we meet there at six thirty?"

I was a little surprised that he didn't offer to pick me up, but then what did I know about going on a date? This would be my first. "Sure. I'll see you there."

He laughed. "Okay, but it's only Monday. I think I'll run into you before then."

I blushed yet again. "Right, right."

Just then the bell rang. We all said a hasty farewell, and went our separate ways to class.

SEVEN

I expected Ruth to be waiting for me at the end of the day. I knew I had some explaining to do. I'd never mentioned Michael to her before, and suddenly we were going on a date. It was kind of a big deal, and Ruth only knew about it because she walked up to me at the right moment. I wasn't sure what her reaction to the news would be, but the fact that she'd sacrificed our plans so I could go out with Michael was a good sign. I hoped.

I saw her standing just inside the main doors, looking distracted, and tugging at some strands of her long, red hair—clearly lost in thought. Ruth was quiet as we walked out of the building toward the parking lot. We'd planned to go to the library to work on our first serious English project, and she was driving. My eco-friendly parents didn't believe that we should own more than one car—the whole carbon footprint thing. They figured I could—and should—walk anywhere I needed to go in Tillinghast, even in the winter.

It irked them that I circumvented their wishes by driving everywhere with Ruth.

I was quiet, too, waiting for her verdict.

"Why didn't you tell me about Michael?" she finally said.

Still unsure how to read her, I tread cautiously. "Tell you what?"

"About your relationship with him."

"Relationship? We've only been in school for a little over a week, and Michael and I have talked a total of maybe five times. Today's the first time that an actual date came up."

"Don't be literal with me, Ellie. You've obviously been talking to him, and you haven't mentioned him even once. And you had plenty of opportunities; we were together all Saturday night."

I had my answer: Ruth was mad. As mad as the reserved Ruth got. I guessed that her anger wasn't from jealousy of my marginal success with a guy, but because I hadn't told her. I knew that the very thought of keeping secrets from each other was beyond her comprehension. In fact, to her, it was tantamount to betrayal. It offended her sense of loyalty.

"I'm sorry. I didn't think there was really much to say."

"I thought we told each other everything. Whether it seems inconsequential or not."

"Ruth, no one knows better than you that I have absolutely no experience with guys. I didn't know if he was just being friendly because we'd both been on that grueling summer program to Guatemala a few years ago. So I didn't really know what to tell you—"

"He was on one of your parents' trips?" She paused to process that little nugget. "So that's why he was staring at us on the first day of school. . . ."

Ruth saw Michael that day. I was shocked that she noticed him but never mentioned him and offended that she thought the only reason he'd stare at me was familiarity. But I was in the hot seat, not Ruth, so I said, "Yeah, our parents do similar kinds of work. He recognized me in the hallway, and it was so awkward because I didn't remember him—"

Ruth's anger couldn't hold. She interrupted me. "I get it, Ellie. Even though I'm still a little mad that you kept it from me, I'm excited for you," she said and sounded like she really meant it. "So, what are you going to wear on Saturday?"

I was forgiven, and Ruth was off and running, mentally culling through my limited wardrobe. My parents were not big believers in amassing goods beyond the absolutely necessary. This dismayed Ruth, who was a secret student of fashion although you'd never know it from her bland school "uniform" of jeans, T-shirts, and sweaters. After listening to Ruth debate the merits of jeans versus skirts, I ventured a question about Michael. One I'd wanted to ask all week, but I'd hesitated to bring up to the very protective Ruth. Until now.

"You don't know anything about him, do you?" I asked, and there was that crimson flush on my cheeks again. "I mean, have you heard anything about Michael's move here?"

"Well, sure, let's see." I could practically see Ruth ticking through her internal file folders on every person in the upper school—another one of her secret hobbies. She collected gossip, but she didn't spread it. At least, not to anyone other than me. She claimed that she culled this information out of necessity rather than true interest; she said that, as we learned in *The Art of War*, which we read for history last year, we needed to "know our enemies." We'd had enough unpleasantness with the popular crowd and wannabes for her taste. Again, part of her protective personality—for herself and me.

"His family moved to Tillinghast this summer. He plays football and is supposedly amazing. That is what the new football coach has been saying, anyway. All the different groups of guys are friendly with him—the football players, the soccer guys, even the stoners—but he hasn't latched on to one group. He seems to prefer his own company, by his choice, not anyone else's. Oh, and he's smart. Scary smart, I hear."

Blush notwithstanding, I plunged back in with the question I really wanted to ask. "Has he dated anyone?"

"No." She laughed. "A couple of girls have crushes on him already, but I haven't heard about him paying any particular attention to anyone." She paused and smiled at me. "Until now."

I smiled back. My private little connection with Michael had suddenly become real.

By the end of the week, I'd grown sick of talking about what I should wear on my date. Ruth had torn through my closet in frustration, judging my collection of dark-colored jeans, cords, sweaters, T-shirts, and tops completely unsuitable. She then steered me through her own closet, with its rarely worn but definitely cooler mix of casual clothes. But none of them worked on my slimmer, taller body. Desperate, Ruth finally dragged me to the mall—a place my parents frowned upon as a sad temple to materialism—looking for something "date-like," whatever that meant.

There was only one good thing about Ruth's mad quest for the perfect date outfit. Between that and my regular schoolwork, I was so distracted that I barely had any time to think about the purpose for all this madness. So by the time 6:30 on Saturday evening rolled around, and my parents dropped me off in front of the Odeon with eyebrows arched at the fact that Michael didn't pick me up, I wasn't even that nervous.

I stood at the Odeon's doors all by myself watching the clock tick off fifteen minutes. Those fifteen minutes gave me ample time to review all my conversations with Michael and cringe over my awkward comments, to wonder what on earth we'd talk about, and to triple-guess my Ruth-approved outfit. I started to feel so anxious that I wondered if I should leave.

But then Michael rounded the corner. When I saw him wearing a pair of khakis and a button-down, I was glad to have worn the vintage blazer, long-sleeve black J. Crew top, and skinny black pants that Ruth had insisted upon. And I was really, really happy that I had stayed.

"I'm so sorry to keep you waiting, Ellie," Michael said as he handed me a beautiful, gold-foil gift bag. "This isn't an excuse, but I hope it explains my delay."

I took the bag with a small, cautious smile. I reached inside and slid out a box of expensive chocolate truffles with a cinnamon center. I couldn't believe it. Over the course of the week, Michael had casually asked me about my favorite candy, and I'd named my dream treat. I never imagined that he'd get it for me.

"I can't believe you remembered."

"You didn't tell me how hard these were to come by in Tillinghast."

"I can't believe you found them in town at all. I've only ever had them abroad in duty-free shops when I traveled with my parents for those summer trips."

He smiled sheepishly. "I didn't find them in Tillinghast exactly."

"Please don't tell me that you went too far out of your way."

"Let's just say that the gift shop in the big hotel in Bar Harbor carries a really nice selection of candy." He took me by the hand and said, "Come on, we don't want to miss the movie, do we?"

EIGHT

The movie and dinner couldn't have gone better if I'd scripted them myself. The movie was a perfect choice, enough action and philosophy to satisfy us both, but no embarrassing love scenes. I had enough trouble concentrating on the movie given that my arm kept brushing up against Michael's, without having to deal with some on-screen love interest. The diner where we had burgers and fries afterward seemed somehow transformed into a French bistro straight out of one of the movie scenes. And we talked easily all night.

Over a shared dessert, we playfully debated some more foreign films. As we finished both the chocolate cake and our cheerful dispute, he said, "God, I'm glad you're in Tillinghast."

I felt my cheeks burn bright red. I wasn't sure how to take his statement, so I pushed the chocolate cake crumbs around the plate and said, "You are?"

"I mean it's so great to find someone in this small town who's smart and interested in the world beyond Tillinghast. Someone who's traveled to the same kind of obscure places and who's dealt with the same kind of single-minded parents."

The way Michael said "someone" made me hesitate. Was he happy to have found just anyone with whom he could connect? Or was he happy to have found *me*?

As if he knew what I was thinking, he said, "I'm so glad to have found you here, of all places. Imagine seeing you again in Tillinghast after first meeting you in rural Guatemala."

I smiled and looked up. "Even if I can't remember you from Guatemala?" I'd tried and tried to conjure up even one image of him from Guatemala, but couldn't. It was like a wall in my head that I couldn't scale or peer around no matter how hard I tried.

He smiled back. "Even if I was forgettable in Guatemala."

We laughed over my forgetfulness, and I was hugely relieved. Up until now, we'd managed to skirt the issue of Guatemala and my strange amnesia about him. But I'd always felt awkward about it. Not anymore.

As he helped me into my jacket after dinner, I thought

about how I loved what I saw in Michael. He was funny, chivalrous, and thoughtful, always opening the door for me and even stopping to help an older woman struggling to cross the street in between the theater and diner. He was obviously well-traveled, and really bright. He had only one flaw: He seemed too good to be true. In fact, he was so comfortable it made me wonder whether he'd been on tons of dates before.

We walked toward the diner door, and I wondered if I should call my parents for a ride. After all, Michael hadn't said anything about driving me home, and he did ask me to meet him at the movies. Maybe he didn't have a car, and I didn't want to be presumptuous.

I pulled out my cell phone, and started to dial. He asked, "Who are you calling?"

"My parents."

"Do you always call them to report in midway through a date?" he said with a laugh.

"No. Well, I don't go on dates—" I turned bright red at my unintentional confession. "What I mean is I don't have to 'report in' or anything—"

He laughed. "I'm only kidding, Ellie. If you need to call your parents for some reason, by all means, please do."

"I just thought we were probably heading home and I should call them for a ride."

"A ride? I was hoping to drive you home myself."

"You were?"

"Of course. If that's all right with you?"

I nodded happily.

Michael was quiet as he helped me into his parents' navy Prius and headed toward my house. I wondered if I'd done or said something wrong, and tried to fill the void with chatter. But Michael seemed perfectly content driving in near-silence, with one hand on the wheel and the other nearly touching mine.

He pulled up in front of my house. Our little white Victorian, with its whimsically painted Kelly green trim and wide front porch that my parents had resuscitated from demolition, looked especially inviting. The warm lights coming from the kitchen were a sure sign that my parents were waiting up for me.

"Would you like to come in?" I wasn't sure if I should ask, but it seemed the normal thing to do. Plus I was nervous. I'd never been on a date before—let alone kissed a guy—and I figured that might come next. Part of me hoped it would, even though I didn't have the slightest idea what to do.

"Maybe it'd be better if I came in and saw your parents next time. I'd kind of like to keep you all to myself tonight."

The words "next time" had such a sweet ring to me. They were a reassurance of sorts that he had enjoyed our evening, even if he'd grown quiet. I put my hand on the car door handle and said, "Until 'next time,' then."

Michael reached across me and gently took my hand off the handle. "Are we done with 'this time' so soon?" If his voice hadn't cracked when he asked the question, he might have seemed smooth, too smooth. Instead, he just seemed endearing.

I didn't want the date to end either, even though I was anxious. I shook my head and looked down.

With his free hand, Michael traced my cheek and lips, and rested his hand at the back of my neck, lifting my face to his. He slipped his other hand around the small of my back and drew me close. So close I could feel his breath on my skin.

He leaned in to kiss me, and I surrendered. His lips were soft and gentle at first, as gentle as he'd been with me all night. I responded intuitively, following his lead as he grew more persistent.

Slowly, so slowly, he parted my lips with his tongue. The delicate, but powerful, motion took my breath away. I waited as he ran his tongue around the tip of my own and then along the ridge of my upper teeth with an alluring deliberation. The movement sent shivers down my spine.

I wanted to provoke the same reaction in him. Tentatively, I touched his tongue with the tip of mine and then sought out his upper teeth. Mimicking his motions, I ran my tongue along the ridge, but it was razor-sharp. I cried out in pain, as my blood filled both of our mouths.

Instinct told me to pull back and I started to apologize, but Michael grabbed hold of me. Just like that, the intensity heightened. His kisses became more and more demanding, and I found myself swept away by his ardor and my own. My pain did nothing to lessen my desire. The feeling was so new . . . but the rush felt almost familiar. Like I was in one of my nightly dreams, flying high above the town below.

Panting, Michael broke away first. We looked into each other's pale, pale eyes, and I saw a hunger in his matched only by my own. I never knew that kissing could be like this. Not even from the movies.

"I think we should stop," he said.

I'd never dreamed of feeling so much, so quickly. I didn't want it to stop. As if in a dream, I said, "No, I don't want to." And I reached for him.

"Yes, Ellie." He placed his hand on mine to keep me at bay.

Still, I wanted more. "Please, Michael." I pressed forward, against the pressure of his hand.

He pushed me back into my seat. Gently, but it was enough to break the spell.

What on earth had come over me? I was mortified at

my aggressive behavior, and embarrassed by his rejection. I recoiled into the far corner of my seat, as far away from his spurning as I could get. But it wasn't far enough. More than anything in the world, I wanted out of that car.

As I reached for the door handle, he grabbed my hand. "Ellie, please believe me when I say that I'm stopping only because we are meant to be together. And this is just the beginning."

I tried to wrench free of his grip. "Don't bother letting me down easy, Michael. I may be inexperienced, but I wasn't born yesterday."

Michael locked his hands around mine. "Please, Ellie."

I met his gaze as if I understood—and agreed with— his excuses. But I nodded only so he would release my hands. Once free, I opened the door and ran from the car. From him.

NINE

I tossed and turned for hours after our date. I was restless, both mentally and physically. My mind raced with replays of our evening together, while my body was plagued by a longing for Michael that even memories of his pushing me away couldn't shake.

When I finally fell asleep sometime near dawn, I sunk back into my recurring dream. It started out on its normal course; I flew out of my bedroom window and into town. I made my usual pause at the village green and town church before heading out to the sea.

Before I could reach the rocky cliffs bordering the ocean, I noticed a clear blue light coming from a house near the beach—a serious departure from my dream's customary path. It was the only visible illumination in the otherwise black landscape. Somehow my body knew precisely how to perform, and I streamlined my limbs to gain speed.

Within seconds, I neared the street and circled the

perimeter of the house. I noted a few lit lamps in the empty family room and kitchen, but this was not the illumination I sought. Although the rest of the house seemed dark, I soon realized that the blue light came from an upstairs bedroom—Michael's bedroom.

Michael sat at his desk, staring out at the sea. I couldn't see the source of the blue light, so I flew close to his window. He looked so handsome and contemplative that I wanted to touch him. Even though he didn't see me, I reached out my hand for him. But then the wind kicked up and begged for my attention. I watched as it whipped through the copse of apple trees in Michael's backyard, violently rustling the branches and late summer leaves.

For a moment, I left Michael behind, and followed my undeniable compulsion to rise. My head tilted upward toward the sky, and my shoulders broadened as if I had wings unfurling. My eyes closed as the wind swept me into its arms, and the sky tugged me gently toward the heavens. I surrendered to the joyous feeling of flight and freedom.

But then my body lurched downward, tangling me in the apple trees. I looked down, expecting to see hands clutched at my ankles or sinuous branches wrapped around my calves. But there was nothing. Nothing except the earth keeping its hold.

* * *

The next thing I remembered was the phone ringing. I sat up with a start, surprised to see bright sunlight streaming through the slats of my window shades. What time was it? I groped for my clock, and couldn't believe it was almost ten o'clock. I never slept this late, even on the weekends. I just wasn't wired for it.

As I grabbed my things for the shower, I noticed the caller ID alert on my cell phone. I checked and saw that I had messages from Ruth and Michael. I could guess what Ruth was dying to talk about, but what did Michael want? To offer his sugarcoated excuses again? I didn't think I could face either one just yet.

Instead, I made my way down the hall to my bathroom. I hoped a long, hot shower would help wash away some of the dream and the thoughts of Michael that started to creep back into my consciousness. After I dried my face and moved on to the thicket of my hair, I heard my mom call from downstairs.

"Ellie? Ellie, honey, are you up?"

I cracked open the bathroom door, and called back, "Yes, Mom."

"Good, we need to leave in fifteen minutes." Although my parents weren't sticklers for church every Sunday morning, they did insist that we serve at a local soup kitchen on Sundays. They believed God was best worshipped by action, not words.

"I'll be ready."

So, there would be no long, hot shower this morning. But maybe a morning at the soup kitchen was exactly what I needed. Hard reality would wipe Michael right out of my head.

I raced to get ready, but my brush kept getting stuck in a particularly dense knot in the back. I tried to separate out the tethered strands one by one with a comb. When the knot refused to budge, I realized that something was holding the hairs together. Finally, I shook the object free to the floor and bent down to pick it up. It was a single leaf from an apple tree.

I lifted the leaf up to the bathroom light to be absolutely certain. There was no denying what it was. I couldn't remember the last time I'd been anywhere near an apple tree. Except in my dream. Last night.

TEN

I successfully avoided Michael on Monday and Tuesday. He tried to get my attention as I left a few classes, but I feigned obliviousness. I did not want to relive the humiliation of our date, and my raw need for him toward the end. In the light of day, walking around school, it was hard to believe I'd actually acted that way. Just to be safe, I kept Ruth by my side as a shield. She thought I was making too big a deal out of it, even after she heard what happened, but she supported me. As always.

By Wednesday, I didn't see Michael waiting anywhere. At first, I experienced overwhelming relief that I could stop the playacting. But as the day progressed, I couldn't help but feel disappointed. Even though I was still cringing over my actions and Michael's response, I was drawn to him.

Following an after-school meeting on Wednesday, I walked to the town library by myself. Ruth's yearbook meeting was running even later, so she couldn't drive me.

And truth be told, I looked forward to the short stroll in the crisp autumn air—alone. I needed some solitude to clear my mind of the all-encompassing thoughts of Michael and refocus on my neglected schoolwork.

I rounded a lazy bend in the road and spied the library a few blocks off. The library was a marble and granite confection from the eighteen hundreds, when the prominent millinery families still had money to spend on Tillinghast, and its founders had spared no expense on an entry staircase worthy of the building's grandeur. I was just about to walk up its imposing steps when I spotted Michael's car idling in the no parking zone in front of the library. Did he know I was coming?

Quickly starting up the stairs, I kept my head down. I reached out for the huge brass door to pull it open. I began to let out a sigh of relief, when I felt a hand on my upper arm.

"Please, Ellie. Just listen to me for a second."

I couldn't pretend any longer. Turning around, I stared into Michael's pale green eyes. Keeping hold of my arm, he whispered to me in a rush, as if he was scared I'd run off.

"Ellie, I've never been more certain about anything than my feelings for you. In fact, they're so strong that they shock me sometimes. I pushed you away the other night because I wanted you too much. And I was afraid I'd scare you if I gave in to my feelings."

Michael stared into my eyes as he spoke, never wavering in his gaze or his words. His confidence made me feel doubly mortified. How could I have refused to give him a chance to explain over the past few days? I broke our connection and looked down at my feet. I wasn't sure I deserved his persistence.

He put his finger under my chin and lifted my face so he could look into my eyes. But I kept them averted. "Ellie, you did nothing to be ashamed of on Saturday night. I wanted you, too. I slowed us down only because I wanted things to be perfect between us."

My cheeks turned bright pink, and I continued staring down at the ground. "Me too, Michael. I was just so embarrassed. I've never behaved like that—felt like that—in my life, and then to have you—"

He placed his finger over my lips and whispered. "Shh. Ellie, I've never behaved or felt like that either. And I'm sorry I pushed you away."

"Really?" I asked without shifting my gaze, too scared that if I looked at him he might just disappear like a character from one of my dreams or suddenly rebuff me again. Once again, Michael seemed just too good to be true.

"Really. Can we start again?"

Finally, I looked into his eyes. I smiled sheepishly and said, "I'd like that."

Michael led me down the steep library steps to his waiting car and opened the door for me. As I waited for him to get into the driver's side, I noticed a couple walking up the stairs to the library. Their attractiveness caught my attention at first, and then I realized that I recognized the girl. It was Missy. She was walking very close to a tall, blond guy who definitely wasn't Charlie, the senior I thought she'd been seeing since last year.

The driver's door opened, and Michael slid in. Before he said a single word, he leaned in to kiss me. The chaste action was a far cry from the night before, but the gesture helped assuage my fears and drove out all thoughts of Missy and whomever she might be dating these days.

"Do you mind if we drive down to the ocean? There's a great spot where we can watch the sunset," Michael asked.

"Sure, that sounds great."

To my relief, Michael launched into safe topics like homework and classes during the drive to the shore. I hardly noticed the change in scenery because I was so engrossed in Michael. And happy to be back with him.

We pulled to the side of the road and got out of the car. Michael had parked at the flat top of a steep cliff that overlooked a beach. I crept over to the edge and looked down onto a picturesque cove that I'd never seen before, not in all my years living in Tillinghast.

"What is this place?"

"It's called Ransom Beach."

The sun was just beginning to descend. Its fall cast purple shadows over the white sand beach below. Michael grabbed my hand and started to lead me down a jagged trail cut almost invisibly into the cliff face. He directed us so expertly down the precipitous path that I realized he must have come this way many times before. In minutes, we scuttled down the rocks onto the sand where the cove's huge, craggy boulders wrapped around us like a cold embrace.

Michael put his arm around my shoulder to shelter me from the moaning wind, as we watched the sun. We made small talk about how pretty it was, and then he asked quietly, "I'd like to talk about last night, if that's okay."

I stiffened and then tried to lighten the mood a little. "We haven't talked about it enough already?"

He laughed. "Almost. I want to talk to you about the reason I think we respond so strongly to each other, Ellie."

"You do?"

"Have you ever sensed that you were different from other people?"

I had to laugh again, and not just because he was acting

so melodramatic. Looking up at him, I answered honestly. "If by 'different' you mean more awkward than most people, then yes."

"Awkward? You're kidding, right?"

I shook my head. Even though I found my gawkiness funny sometimes, I definitely wasn't kidding.

"If you're really serious, then you've got to understand that you are the only one who sees you that way. Everyone else sees you as smart and intimidating and worldly and pretty."

I almost snorted with laughter, but then stopped myself. "Yeah, right."

"Piper and Missy have been really friendly to you lately, haven't they?"

"Yes . . ." I wondered how he knew and where he was going with his question.

"But they still ignore you sometimes, don't they?"

"Yes."

"Idiots like Piper and Missy seek you out at the same time they ostracize you because you scare them. They don't know what to do with someone like you. Someone attractive and bright and completely uninterested in their games. Someone that they sense is different and special, but they don't know in what way."

I was genuinely shocked. "Come on, Michael. I already

like you; you don't have to flatter me. I am not different and special." My parents had worked long and hard to make me feel smart and important and loved, but at the same time, were always careful to remind me that I was just a regular girl, just like everyone else. With responsibilities to other people and the planet.

"If only you could see how beautiful and unique you really are," Michael said, and leaned in to kiss me.

The howl of the wind and the increasing chill receded as I lost myself to him. He wrapped himself around me and kissed me with rapidly growing intensity. Just like when we were in the gym and his car, I could only see and think and feel Michael.

Gently, so gently, he pressed me back into the sand. His kisses grew more insistent, and I enjoyed his mounting excitement. In a familiar motion, he parted my lips and ran his tongue along my tongue. He swept his tongue back into his own mouth and ran it along his own teeth, and I then felt his tongue lightly touch my own.

A metallic taste flooded my mouth. Michael had caused the slightest drop of his blood to drip onto my tongue. The sand and the wind and the cove disappeared, and I experienced a powerful flash—much stronger than I'd ever experienced before. I saw myself on that first day of school, walking down the hallway with Ruth after the episode with her and Missy. I watched as I whipped my head in Michael's direction, and I couldn't believe how I appeared. My pale skin and eyes looked striking against the sleek blackness of my hair, and my long, lithe body was outlined in a glowing light. As seen through Michael's eyes, I was indeed beautiful, almost ethereally so.

Just then, the upper school hallway faded, and I saw another, more disconcerting image of myself. I watched as I elevated to Michael's second-floor bedroom window and stretched out my hand in an invitation to flight. It was a scene from my dream.

I drew back from Michael's kiss, and the image disappeared. Pushing myself up from the sand, I asked, "What was that? How did you know—"

"How did I know that you saw images like that? That you get insights into other people's thoughts and feelings and baggage?"

"Yes." I could barely breathe.

"How did I know that you dream of flying? And that, last night, you flew by my bedroom window in your dream?"

"Yes."

"Ellie, I told you that you are different. We are different. And that difference means we are meant for each other."

Eleven

Different—what did Michael mean by different? I was too freaked out to ask. I was also too terrified—of him, the images, even myself—to stand there next to him on that remote beach as darkness fell around us. I felt betrayed, too. Had he orchestrated the whole reconciliation just so he could bring me here and frighten me? And how did he know about my flashes? About my dreams? Something was off. I backed away from him and headed toward the rocky pathway leading to the road.

Michael hurried after me. "I'm sorry, Ellie. I didn't mean to scare you."

I turned around and said, "Well, you did." Then I kept moving up the path.

I felt his hand as he reached out for me. "Come on, let me help you back up the trail."

Keeping my hands glued to my sides and marching forward, I said, "No thanks, you've 'helped' enough. I'll make my own way." I didn't want him touching me just then. What if he could transmit more of his thoughts and images to me—or, worse, obtain more of my thoughts and images?

The sun had almost sunk beneath the horizon, and the pathway was getting really hard to see. I trudged ahead as if I knew what I was doing—and where I was going. As I made my way along the narrow path, I heard some rocks slide down the steep cliff face. The sound startled me, and I lost my confidence and my footing. I started to slip, and Michael grabbed me just in time.

I sat for a moment to catch my breath. Since I didn't experience any weird flashes as he pulled me up, I figured that I should accept his help the rest of the way. I walked with his hand on my arm until we finally reached the peak. There, I tried to shake off his hand so I could walk to the car on my own. But he held tight.

"Ellie, look at me."

I didn't want to look at him. As we had hiked up that treacherous path, I had thought about what had passed between us. Whether or not the sensations were real—and I wasn't ready to tackle that just yet—I was furious. How dare he bring me to such an isolated, even dangerous, spot to inflict all this on me? And I didn't want my anger to soften when I looked into his eyes, which I suspected it might.

"Please, Ellie."

I kept my gaze fixed on the ground. "Why should I, Michael? You dragged me out here to this remote beach to scare me with some kind of game."

"Game?"

"Yes."

"You think that the images I shared with you were some kind of game?" He sounded shocked, even a little mad. I didn't dare look at his face.

"Yes." In truth, I wasn't sure. I'd experienced enough flashes, visions, or whatever you wanted to call them, of my own to suspect that they might be real. But I didn't want to admit it out loud to him—because then I'd have to face it. And I desperately wanted to be regular, like my parents had always told me I was. I'd never had any trouble thinking of myself that way until right now. I did not want to be different, especially not in this weird way.

"They were no trick, Ellie. You are different. We are different."

"We are not. I don't know how you did what you did, but there's nothing different about either of us."

I felt Michael stare at me, and I couldn't keep my eyes averted any longer. Even though it was fairly dark, I could see the startling greenness of his eyes. I refused to let them unnerve me, so I met his gaze. He released my hand. Then, very deliberately, he walked to the edge of the cliff and looked out at the ocean.

"Michael, what are you doing?" I was fuming, but I didn't want him to do anything crazy.

Twisting toward me, he asked, "Are you so sure that your flying is just part of a dream? That you are just a regular girl?"

When I didn't answer, Michael turned back to the sea. He stood frozen for a moment, a black silhouette against the remnants of the simmering crimson sky. For a second, I thought he wanted a moment alone, to cool off. So I walked away from him, in the direction of the car, and then turned to see if he followed.

But Michael hadn't followed me. He hadn't even looked back at me. Instead, in that moment, he stretched out his arms and dove off the cliff.

I lunged for him, but I was too far away. Only the precipice stopped me. Frantic, I dropped to my hands and knees and crawled to the very edge. I scanned the cliff and beach below, but could make out nothing but the blue-gray rocks and the white sand. And then I screamed.

Within seconds, the shock subsided and the obvious occurred to me. I needed to go back down there to search the cliff side and beach for signs of Michael. He could be hurt, or worse, given the sixty-foot drop. The very thought of "worse" started me crying. I felt so guilty, as if my lack of faith in him had pushed him over.

But tears wouldn't bring him back. So I wiped my face and struggled to my feet. Just as I was about to head down the path, I felt someone tap my shoulder. I turned around, thinking that some passerby had heard my screams. I welcomed the help. But I was wrong.

TWELVE

It was Michael.

Michael. Alive. Unhurt.

I could have killed him.

"How could you do that to me?" I yelled.

He had the audacity to smile. "Do what? Fly?"

"Trick me!"

I spun around, away from him and toward the car. Of course he had tricked me. The pieces all fit together. He had brought me to this secluded spot with this whole scheme mapped out to make me believe some crazy fantasy about our shared "difference," whatever that was. And as a last-ditch attempt to convince me, he staged a "flight," really a premeditated jump into some cliff-side niche he obviously knew well, followed by a "magical" reappearance. Why he had gone to all the trouble, I didn't know. Clearly, he didn't need to resort to sleight of hand to get me.

"Boy, this sure isn't going the way I'd hoped," I heard him mutter to himself.

I kept walking.

"Ellie, it was no trick. Surely you must know that the only way I'd survive a leap like that is by flying. I thought you needed to see the truth to believe what I've been telling you."

I stood by the passenger car door, waiting for him to open the lock with his keys. I didn't look at him or speak. I could see that any effort would be of no use; he was going to stick with his story regardless. The last thing in the world I wanted to do was sit alone in a car with him, but I had no choice. I wanted to go home.

He kept on trying to explain himself—"ourselves," he kept repeating—on the ride. But I literally couldn't hear him. I clung to my anger at him as a way of blocking him out. Of blocking out whatever feelings I still had for him and whatever truth might lie deep within his words.

I didn't bother to say good-bye as I got out of the car. Instead, I ran to my front door and closed it behind me. The compulsion to race up the stairs to my bedroom and bury myself under my quilt was strong. I just wanted to forget—about the night, about Michael, about all the weirdness—and awaken to a fresh, new day. But my parents were waiting for me in the kitchen.

"Where have you been, Ellspeth?" my dad asked in an alarmed voice I'd never heard from him before. And he used "Ellspeth"—which he never, ever did.

"At the library."

"Really?" Now it was my mom's turn to use a totally foreign, troubled tone.

"Really."

"Is there anything you want to tell us, Ellspeth?" It was my dad's turn again.

"No," I answered. But as I uttered my denial, I remembered that I had told them that I'd be at the library after school with Ruth. And I never called Ruth to tell her that I wouldn't be there, that I'd be with Michael instead.

I knew what my mom would say before she said it. "Then why did Ruth call here over two hours ago looking for you—from the library?"

I gave the only excuse that I could in the circumstances, even though it created its own host of problems. "I was at the library, Mom. But with Michael, not with Ruth. And then we left to get a cup of coffee."

"The boy from the other night? The boy from Guatemala?" my mom asked.

"Yes."

My parents exchanged a glance I couldn't read.

"Ellspeth Faneuil, you explicitly told us you would be at the library with Ruth. You know better than to leave the library with someone else and not inform us. Especially since it was with a boy we haven't laid eyes on for three years," my mom said, scolding me for the first time I could recall.

"I'm really sorry. I should have called you."

"Yes, you should have. You should have turned on your cell phone, at least," she said.

"Why didn't you, Ellie?" My dad sounded so hurt that it brought tears to my eyes, for the second time that night.

"I just forgot, Dad."

My dad sighed. "Oh, Ellie, if you only knew how important you were, you wouldn't scare us like this or place yourself in jeopardy. You are so special, not just to us, but—" What on earth was my dad saying? Calling me "special" went against everything they'd taught me.

My mom uncharacteristically interrupted him. "What Dad means is that we love you and we want you to be safe. We thought that we had fostered a trust among us, but we can see that the teenage years are putting that to the test. You are going to have to be honest with us from now on, is that clear?"

"Yes, Mom." At that moment, I really meant it. I'd do anything to avoid seeing that wounded look on either of their perfect faces. They looked like they'd aged ten years in that one evening.

They stood up and gave me a hug. The squeeze reminded me that my body ached in exhaustion from all the evening's tumult. I yearned for sleep.

"Do you mind if I head up to bed?" I asked.

"Of course not, Ellie." My dad gave me a kiss good night, and then smiled. "There's just one more thing."

"Sure, Dad."

"We're going to need to reacquaint ourselves with this Michael."

THIRTEEN

I expected that rest would elude me even though my body desperately craved sleep. I guessed that thoughts of Michael and the cove and his cliff-dive would prevent my eyes from closing at all. But the moment I crawled under my quilt and laid down on my pillow, I was out.

Well, out to this world, anyway. Instead, I entered the familiar world of my recurring dream. I awoke in that world with a stronger urge to fly than ever. The impulse propelled me out of my bedroom window and onto my usual route. I soared through Tillinghast's old cobblestone streets with new speed and reckless abandon. Although I made the customary stop at the village green with its whitewashed church gaping at me like some cyclopic eye, it was quicker than ever. I had the feeling that there was somewhere else I needed to be.

Before heading to the shore like I usually did, I followed

the blue light coming from a house near the beach. From my last dream, I knew this was Michael's house. Although I remembered what had gone on between us earlier that day in the real world, the knowledge did not lessen my desire to see him in this dreamscape. I didn't feel mad at him anymore, just peaceful and excited to be with him.

I went immediately to the second floor bedroom where the light came from—Michael's bedroom. As before, he sat at his desk, staring out at the sea, his blond hair bright against the darkness. I flew close to his window, but unlike my last dream, the wind didn't compete for my attention to Michael. I reached out my hand for him.

This time, Michael saw me. He stretched out his arm and clasped my hand with his. With that motion, he lifted out of his window and floated in the air by my side. It all seemed so natural and effortless that we didn't even need to speak. We smiled at each other and set out.

At first, we just flew around the sleeping streets of Tillinghast. Darting in between stores and homes and campus buildings, we reveled in the experience of flying together. He pushed me to climb higher, and I dared him to race me down the streets. We laughed at the sheer thrill of it, and I wished that real life could be this easy.

But then Michael took my hand and led me away from

Tillinghast toward the coast. In my dreams, I'd often flown along the shore, but Michael guided me on a route unknown to me. I gaped in awe as we sped past huge razor-edged rocks and pebbly sand beaches and enormous white-capped ocean waves.

And then he stopped. As I peered down, I realized that I had been here before—by car earlier in the day. We had arrived at the cliff overlooking Ransom Beach.

Slowly, we lowered ourselves to the ground. I studied the setting. It was the darkest hour of the night and the moon was only a quarter full, yet I could see every rock and every blade of grass as if it were midday. Better, in fact. I was really starting to like this dream world.

Even though standing on that flat cliff top reminded me of my earlier anger and fear, it didn't shake the sense of calm and delight that pervaded this idyllic dream. I was curiously detached from my rage. Real life only crept in for a moment as I silently wished I could bottle the peace and use it whenever Piper and Missy really got to me.

Michael strode to the very edge of the cliff. Strangely, I felt compelled to join him. As I walked toward him, my feet felt heavy, almost leaden, after the ease and lightness of flying. Michael smiled at me, as if he understood that walking had become foreign to me after all the flying, and

offered his arm. I grabbed on to it tightly and followed
him back to the precipice. Somehow I knew what we were
about to do, and I welcomed it.

We stretched out our arms and dove.

The wind whipped against my face as we plunged
headlong down the sixty-foot cliff face. Jagged rocks and
smooth-edged boulders whizzed right past me, but I wasn't
scared; I was exhilarated. Anyway, I knew that, if it got to
be too much, I could always wake up.

Just before we hit the sand headfirst, we leveled off. We
floated down the remaining few inches and landed feet-
first in the cove, our hands still locked together. In the
hazy moonlight, the white sand of the cove shimmered
against the blackness of the sea. I was so happy Michael
had brought me back to Ransom Beach. It occurred to me
that perhaps that had been his intention earlier that day—
to share this beautiful spot with me.

"It was my intention. In part." He spoke as if answering
my thoughts. Or had I said my thoughts aloud?

"I realize that now. I am so sorry that I got mad and cut
our visit short."

"Don't be sorry, Ellie. It's my fault. I had another intention, one you weren't ready for."

"What do you mean?"

"I wanted to show you something. But it was too much, too soon."

I didn't respond. I knew what he was going to say next, but I didn't want him to say it. I wanted to remain in this tranquil moment, happy with Michael and this place. But I knew he couldn't let it go—wouldn't let it go—once he started, and I knew his words would shatter the serenity.

"I wanted to show you what we are."

I shook my hand free of his. "Michael, I told you already. There's nothing to show."

"Ellie, think about it. The flying, the insights we have about others, and the power of blood. Especially the blood."

I felt myself getting mad at him again. "And exactly what does this bizarre equation equal?"

"I think—" He stopped as if the words were hard, even for him. "I think that we're vampires."

Even I hadn't guessed his ludicrous theory, and I was torn between laughing and hitting him. I opted for laughing. "Come on, Michael, that's ridiculous. And anyway, this is just a dream."

"This isn't a dream, Ellie. Don't you remember the apple tree leaf caught in your hair from your last 'dream'?"

I didn't want to hear any more, so I willed myself to

wake up. The cove started to blur, and I could feel myself fade away.

Before I totally disappeared, I heard Michael call out. His voice was muffled and faint as if from a far distance, but I swear he said, "When you leave your house tomorrow morning for school, I promise that I'll be waiting for you. That way you'll know that this is not a dream."

FOURTEEN

I sat up in my bed. The quilt slipped off my shoulders, but sun streamed through my bedroom windows and warmed me up. The clock flashed seven A.M. Only twenty minutes to get ready before my mom drove me to school, so I had to move fast. I was glad I didn't have too much time to think.

Racing around, I washed my face and brushed my hair. I threw on some blush and mascara and pulled my hair back in a ponytail. Jeans and a sweater would have to suffice, since I didn't have the luxury of rifling through my closet for something more interesting. I could already hear my mom calling up to me.

Wheat toast with raspberry jam sat waiting for me on the kitchen table, along with a tall glass of orange juice. My mom hurried me along as she did every other morning; she liked to be in her office first thing. She didn't mention the lie about the library, and I felt relieved that she didn't seem upset anymore. We each grabbed our bags and headed for the front door.

Just before she pulled the door open, I realized that I had left my English paper on the desk in my bedroom. I told her that I'd meet her in the car, and I ran upstairs to grab the paper. As I dashed back down the steps, I heard voices on the front porch. I opened the front door to see my mom chatting away—with Michael.

I stopped. Why was he here? I spotted the gift basket in his hands, and I surmised that this was a peace offering for his stunt—a way of buttering up my parents. Michael's outfit—parent-friendly khakis and a rugby shirt— confirmed my suspicions, and made me wish I'd had more than twenty minutes to get myself ready.

My mom turned to me. "Look, dearest, your friend Michael brought us a present. Homemade breads." To him, she probably sounded sweet, but I knew from the cold way she said "your friend" that the bread hadn't won her over. She knew that it was I who had acted badly last night—not Michael—but I'm sure she blamed him in part, for being a bad influence. My mom was way tougher than she looked, way tougher than my dad, in fact. "You must have been up all night making these. After all, you guys got back pretty late from the library." The last dig was for both our benefits.

Michael didn't look in my direction, but kept his focus

on my mom. "Mrs. Faneuil, I have to confess that the present really comes from my mother. She said that I should deliver it to you with her regards."

"How nice of her. Please pass along my thanks." She paused. "And please tell her that we should get together soon. It's been a long, long time."

"I'll do that. In fact, she mentioned the same thing. That it's been too long."

Deftly, Michael turned the talk to our time together in Guatemala. I listened as they recalled people and events on which I drew a complete blank. He and I had talked about the gaps in my memory, so I didn't feel uncomfortable with their conversation, even though it was still troubling. My mom glanced at her watch abruptly and said we should all get going.

Finally, Michael seemed to remember me. He asked, "Mrs. Faneuil, do you mind if I take Ellie to school?"

She paused for a split second that no one but me would have noticed. "No, that's fine. Just be careful with our Ellie."

How embarrassing. "Oh, Mom—"

Michael interrupted me. "I promise, Mrs. Faneuil."

My mom gave me a quick peck on the cheek, and watched as Michael opened the passenger door for me. I slid inside and waited for him, unsure what to say when he closed his door and we were alone.

Once he got in, he leaned over to give me a kiss. His audacity brought the right words to my lips. I wrenched away and said, "Nice move, Michael. Did you think that I'd forget to be mad about the stunt you pulled yesterday just because you brought some bread for my mom?"

To my surprise, he smiled and said, "No, Ellie, I didn't think you'd forgive me just because my mom baked banana bread. You had every right to be angry with me; I know I scared you yesterday."

"Good." I sat back in my seat and crossed my arms in satisfaction. Feeling vindicated, I snuck a look at him to see how he was taking my victory. To my irritation, he was still smiling.

He put the key in the ignition and started the car. "However, I did think you'd forgive me because I kept my promise."

I froze. The only promise Michael had made was to meet me this morning—and he made it in last night's dream. I crossed my arms tightly across my chest. How could he know about that promise unless he could invade my dreams—or unless the dream itself was real? And if the dream was real, then so was the flying. And so were the visions. But I couldn't allow myself to play the thoughts out to their ultimate conclusion.

I said nothing as he pulled out of my driveway and onto

the street. We drove for several minutes without talking; my mind was whirring too fast for words. Could Michael really be right?

Then, without averting his eyes from the road, he said, "I told you that the flying wasn't a dream. It only seems that way."

"So your flight at Ransom Beach was real? And the flying in the dream last night was real?" I whispered aloud the awful truth. They weren't really questions. Not anymore. But I was terribly confused. And afraid.

"Yes, Ellie." He reached over and held my hand. "We can fly. But I think it's really hard for our minds to accept that. So when we venture out into the night on our flights—when our bodies are compelled to do what they are designed to do—our minds tell us that those flights are really dreams. Because to process them as actual flights would challenge everything we have ever known." He paused and looked at me. "Does that make any sense?"

"Sort of. But why was I able to wake up in bed this morning and not remember flying back from Ransom Beach last night, if the dreams are real?"

"Probably because your mind wasn't ready to deal with the truth. And if you remembered flying back from Ransom Beach into your bedroom window and sliding into your cozy bed, it might have made your flying undeniably real."

"I don't know if I'm ready to deal with the truth now," I whispered, half to myself.

Michael gripped my hand tighter. "I'll be here with you, helping you."

I gripped his hand back. "Did you go through all this?"

"Yes. But then the truth dawned on me, and I could no longer pretend the flights were dreams." He smiled. "Anyway, now I want them to be real. And you will too. You'll see."

I felt sick to my stomach. This was all too much.

Michael saw the scared look on my face, and paused. He said, "I know it's hard to accept right now but you and I share some extraordinary gifts."

"I don't know that I'd call them 'extraordinary.' Or 'gifts,' for that matter. I think scary curses might be a better word for them."

Michael laughed even though I wasn't really joking. Once he realized that I was serious, he quickly matched my mood. "Believe me, I know they can seem scary at first. But I'll be there to help you. At the beginning, I thought I was the only one with these powers, and it was really lonely."

A troubling thought occurred to me. "Is that why you sought me out? So you wouldn't be alone in all this madness?"

"No, not at all." We were almost at school, and he pulled

the car into a nearly empty parking lot adjacent to the school gym. He stopped the car, reached out for my hands, and said, "Ellie, I sought you out because I was drawn to you on every level. Not just because I saw that you were like me."

I took a good look into his green eyes, and he appeared sincere. I was relieved, but still not totally trusting. We'd been on a roller coaster since the moment we met.

"How did you know that you and I shared these"—I stumbled over the description—"gifts?"

"The first time I saw you, I wasn't sure. You did seem different from everyone else; you had that glow about you. I'm sure you saw it from that flash I sent you. But on our first date, when I tasted your blood, I knew."

"What do you mean?"

"Your blood gave me the whole picture. It showed me your flashes and your flying. I saw that you had the same susceptibility to blood that I do. And it told me that you were trying to act as though it wasn't happening. Instead, you're clinging to this image of a 'regular girl' that your parents have hammered into your head."

"My blood told you all that?"

"Well, I was really listening. But blood can tell you almost anything about a person. Didn't you see that from my blood?"

I blushed, thinking about the image of myself I'd seen when I tasted Michael's blood. I didn't know if I was ready for all this—especially not the "v" word he mentioned last night, which neither of us had referenced this morning—but I couldn't pretend that it was just a dream any longer.

Michael leaned in to kiss me. My apprehension forced me to hesitate for a second. But then he caressed my hand. His touch sent shivers through me, reminding me of how his lips and tongue and blood made me feel. Unable to resist, I moved toward him.

A tap sounded on his window. We jumped apart, and stared out. It was Mr. Morgans, the phys ed teacher, motioning that the bell was about to ring.

Fifteen

Michael and I raced to our respective classes, but not before I agreed to meet him back at his car at the end of the day. The bell finished ringing before I made it to Miss Taunton's classroom, and she wasn't about to let me get away with sneaking in the door.

"Miss Faneuil, you know my rules about tardiness. You owe me a ten-page biography of Jane Austen."

My jaw dropped; she must have been in a really bad mood because her punishments were usually in the five-page range. My astonished expression didn't escape Miss Taunton.

"You don't like that assignment, Miss Faneuil? You are welcome to detention instead."

I rushed to accept the lighter sentence. I could just imagine the look in my parents' eyes if they learned that Michael delivered me late to school to the tune of detention. "No, no, Miss Taunton. I'm happy to learn more about Jane Austen."

"Good, Miss Faneuil, so am I. I'm sure you'll dazzle me with some esoteric piece of information about one of my favorite writers. Now class, let's hear from . . ."

As I walked to my seat in the back of the classroom, I caught Ruth's sympathetic eye. I couldn't imagine how I'd dredge up fresh biographical details about one of the world's most written-about authors, but I had more pressing concerns. Michael and our "gifts," to name a couple.

After I slid into my chair and unzipped my bag, my cell phone quietly vibrated with a text message. The rare occurrence intrigued me; maybe it was Michael. I created a barrier with my bag so I could glance at it. Nothing made Miss Taunton more furious than students checking their cell phones.

I scrolled to the text: *sorry* with a sad face. It was from Ruth.

I was confused. Looking to make sure that Miss Taunton was safely engrossed in grilling another student, I answered. *Why? The Austen bio?*

The cell vibrated back. *No. Your parents.*

Oh, no. Between the confusion of the dream and Michael's unexpected visit this morning, I'd completely forgotten about Ruth's call to my parents last night. I felt terrible. Why should she feel bad about calling my house when I was the one who didn't give her the heads-up about meeting Michael? I wrote back: *My fault. I'm sorry.*

Risking Miss Taunton's wrath, Ruth turned around in her seat and smiled to show that all was well. It made me feel even worse, like I'd betrayed my own family. For years, Ruth and I had shared everything with each other. In the absence of other siblings, we'd become like sisters, with my mom even playing the role of mother to Ruth when she needed it. I should be begging forgiveness for keeping secrets and using Ruth as a cover for my date with Michael. Not vice versa.

Worse, I'd have to continue keeping secrets from her. How could I tell her about the flying and the flashes I got about people? Or the way blood affected me? With good reason, she'd run off to my parents, and they'd have me committed. No, I'd have to explore this with Michael alone, while I spun a fairy tale for Ruth about the normal side of my relationship with him.

Miss Taunton's voice grew shrill as she subjected a poor junior named Jamie and his "inadequate" assessment of Jane Austen to her scrutiny. I reached for my bag to slip my cell phone back inside, when it dawned on me that I might have a few free minutes while Miss Taunton continued with her tirade. Yielding to temptation, I searched Wikipedia for "vampire."

I scrolled through the long entry, and other than some terrifying definitions of blood-sucking, death-dealing vampires, I didn't find any descriptions that sounded like Michael or me. Relief coursed through me; maybe Michael was wrong.

The name Professor Raymond McMaster was quoted extensively on the page. There was a link to the Harvard University webpage with his bio. He was an expert in the history of vampires and other supernatural beings. Some of his academic papers sounded interesting, and I was about to click onto "In search of the real Dracula" when I heard my name.

"Miss Faneuil, am I boring you?"

My head snapped up. Miss Taunton marched toward me. I scrambled to hide the phone under the mound of papers I'd scattered on my desktop. On top, I placed the paper due. She stopped within inches of me and waited for my answer while the class held its collective breath.

"Of course not. I was just rereading the paper we're turning in today."

Miss Taunton looked over my shoulder at the paper in my hand, smiled, and lunged for it. Her hand brushed against mine, and I received a very intense flash. I was in a fussy, formal-looking living room, complete with lace doilies on the end tables and cloyingly flowery wallpaper. For a second, I was disoriented, but then I caught a look in a mirror facing the couch on which I sat. Miss Taunton stared out at me. On her lap was a copy of *Wuthering Heights.* Tears streamed down her face. She was about to turn the page when I heard my name: "Ellie Faneuil."

The sad image faded, and I found myself staring right into Miss Taunton's eyes. I nearly wanted to reach over and pat her hand—her life was that pitiful, that macabre—but then she gave me a sick grin. My stomach lurched, and she said, "Thank you for returning to us, Miss Faneuil. I can see how this paper would be far more interesting than what I have to say about Jane Austen. Why don't you read your paper aloud to the class, since it appears to be so mesmerizing?"

I rose from my chair, ready to be humiliated. My paper was titled "Sex in *Pride and Prejudice.*"

One positive emerged from my mortification in English class. It wiped clean from Ruth's mind the incident from Sunday night. Loyal friend that she was, she stepped forward to defend the teasing I took from my classmates right afterward. By lunchtime, the story had spread to Missy,

Piper, and their lesser lights, and Ruth stood up for me with them, too. No one wanted to believe that I used the word "sex" in the title to denote "gender," no matter how many times Ruth explained it or the fact that they actually heard me read the paper.

I couldn't wait for the school day to end, even though the afternoon presented its own challenges. Mercifully alone, I walked to the still-empty back lot where we'd parked. There stood Michael. He pulled a bunch of perfect red tulips from behind his back and handed them to me.

"Thank you. They're so pretty. Where did you get them?" I asked. They hardly sold flowers in the cafeteria.

"I can fly, can't I?"

I was horrified, and my face must have shown it.

He pulled me into his chest. "I'm sorry, Ellie. I was joking. I drove to the florist shop right down the road."

"Thank goodness." I stayed buried in his chest.

"I figured you needed them today."

I looked up into his face. "Oh, no, you heard about English."

Michael winced. "I think everyone heard."

I groaned and buried my head in my hands. "It really was nothing like everyone is saying," I said, suddenly more embarrassed. At his mischievous smile, I groaned again. "I'll never live this down."

"I have a plan that might take your mind off of it," he said, and opened the car door for me.

As I climbed in, I asked warily, "What's this plan?"

"I think it's time we practiced your flying."

Sixteen

Michael didn't mean that we should take off right there and then. Instead, he took me home, came inside to say hello to my mom, who'd just arrived from work, and stayed to make small talk with her before heading home to do his schoolwork. He did all the things you'd expect from a new boyfriend—except for the plan to meet me at my bedroom window at midnight.

Dinner dragged on and on that night. My parents mentioned Michael a few times, but I was relieved that they seemed appeased by his visits that morning and afternoon. Mostly, I felt antsy; I just wanted to get up to my room and get ready for him. It was amazing that I was so willing to indulge in our strange abilities. I hated being the odd one out. I hated these "gifts" as Michael called them. Until I met him. Whatever these powers were, not having to face them alone was the gift. And tonight we were going to fly together, while wide awake. No more hiding in dreams.

By the time my clock signaled twelve, I had been sitting at my window seat in the dark for nearly a half an hour. I had chosen sweats that could pass for pajamas should I run into my parents before I left, and I had stuffed my bed with pillows to make it look like I was in there asleep. Staring out the window, I willed Michael to appear.

But when he finally arrived, nothing could quite prepare me for the sight of his face floating outside my window. With his blond hair looming white against the black night and his wide grin resembling a jack-o'-lantern's smile, I stifled a scream. Breathing deeply to slow my racing heart, I unlatched the window and prayed that the creaky old windowpanes wouldn't wake up my parents.

"Ready?" Michael asked.

I nodded, even though I was terrified. He stuck his hand through the opening and motioned for me to take hold. My hand was shaking, but I grasped on to him.

Taking a leap of faith like no other, I let Michael wrap his arm around my waist and lift me through the window and into the air. We hovered two stories over the ground, and I clung to his arm like a life preserver. Even though I'd flown before, I'd always believed it to be dream—with no fears, no repercussions. Michael was right; once I understood that it wasn't a dream, everything changed. This experience was entirely different, almost hyper-real.

"Are you all right?" he whispered to me.

Still clinging to his arm, I whispered back, "I think so."

"Okay, let's go." He pulled me tighter and we took off.

I wondered where we were headed, but I couldn't look. Instead, I buried my face in his shoulder. Sensing and hearing the wind as our speed increased, I could barely make out his words. "Ellie, you should really open your eyes. It's an amazing view."

I shook my head. Michael wound his other arm around me.

Other than the wind, we flew in silence. My body began to remember how to fly, and I could feel my shoulders expand and my legs streamline. But then my mind took hold—fear permeated my thoughts—and Michael had to carry me along.

We slowed, and I could feel Michael lower us toward the ground. I peeked out through my formerly hermetically sealed eyes and gasped. We were still a good forty feet off the ground. How high had we been flying? I vowed to keep my eyes shut until I could actually feel the earth beneath my feet.

With a thud, we hit land. Michael removed his arm, and dizzily I fell to the soft grass-covered ground. Rushing to my side, he helped me up with a joke. "You'd think you've never flown before."

I laughed. "I haven't. Not awake, anyway."

"You were awake, you just didn't know it."

"I think that's the problem tonight. I know I'm not sleeping."

I stood up and looked around, my eyes able to see the finest details of the landscape. We were in a flat open field ringed by fir trees. The place seemed safe and secluded, the perfect spot for a first flying date. The very thought gave me pause; what was happening to my life?

"Should we start?" he asked.

"Yes," I said, even though I really didn't want to try. Not only was I scared, but I didn't want to embarrass myself any further in front of Michael.

He said, "When I was first trying, I found it easier to start high and dive down, rather than lift off from the ground. Unfortunately, we don't have that option tonight. This is really the only secure area for practice."

Michael lined me up in front of him. Straightening both of my arms, he positioned them above my head. Then he whispered, "Relax," and stepped back to watch.

I felt like a dork. At first, I could not rise off the grass. But then I followed Michael's advice; I closed my eyes and envisioned myself ascending. I tried to stop analyzing my every move and summon up the sensation from my dreams. With a lurch, my feet lifted up, and I started to fly.

The feeling was different from my dreams, more halting and awkward. A sensation I knew all too well from my daytime life. My instincts competed for my attention, begging me to lengthen my arms and legs as I swooped through the air. When I surrendered to my impulses, I recaptured some of the grace from my "dream" flying.

I began to enjoy myself. I climbed and plunged through the night sky like it was my playground. As I made one particularly steep dive, I noticed Michael on the field below watching me. Instead of sweeping back up before I got too close, I decided to land next to him.

But I didn't quite know how to touch down softly. I landed on my bottom, knocking Michael down in the process. Laying there in the field, we burst into hysterical laughter. I started to wipe my tears away and sit up when he pulled me back down. He kissed me with such force it took my breath away.

I forgot all about the flying and the field. I yielded to his hands as they ran up and down my arms and legs, tracing circles wherever they went. I submitted to his tongue as it explored my lips and mouth and neck with the lightest touch. And then I tasted the blood.

I felt the blood—his blood—course through me. It burned like the wine I'd snuck once at a wedding, making me feel weak and invincible at once. As the blood

surged through me, a breathtaking image seared my consciousness.

He broke away. "Tell me what you saw."

A tiny droplet of blood remained on my lip. I licked it
before answering. I wanted more.

With effort, I said, "I saw a beautiful winged woman."

"Winged?" Michael looked confused.

I closed my eyes and tried to remember the image more
clearly. "Well, she didn't have wings exactly. More like two
arcs of light behind her shoulders."

He nodded, as if that made more sense. "Did you recognize her?"

I suddenly realized who she was. "Yes, it was me."

He smiled. "Do you believe me now that we are special?"

"Yes." I did, even though it went against my parents'
teachings. Whether it was the heady influence of the blood
or the flying or merely his proximity, it didn't matter. I
believed him.

Michael kissed me again. I could feel myself being over-
taken by him. But a tiny, nagging question stood in the way
of being totally engulfed by him. I broke away. "How did
you discover the way blood affected you? I would never
have known unless you showed me."

Even though it was really dark, my newly sharp eyesight allowed me to see him blush. "I took this girl to the

junior prom last year, when we lived in Pittsburgh."

"Yes?" I recoiled a little.

"Well, we kissed at the end of the night and her tongue got cut by my teeth. You know how sharp they are—"

"Yes, I do." I felt sick at the thought of Michael kissing another girl.

"I got the strongest sensation from it, much more powerful than anything I'd seen by touch. I learned something really disturbing about her childhood, something she had never told anyone."

"What was it?"

He hesitated. "Her dad used to hit her mom. They got divorced when she was little, but I got these really clear images from her childhood. I felt so uncomfortable that I couldn't even look her in the eye afterward."

"I'm sorry I made you tell me." Although I wasn't sorry that he couldn't bear to be around her after the incident.

He hugged me. "Don't apologize, Ellie. It's critical that we tell each other everything. Even really unpleasant things, okay?"

"Okay." I paused, weighing whether I should share my "unpleasant" speculation with him. There would never be a better time. "Then I should probably tell you that I think your vampire theory is off the mark. I did a little research, and I don't think we fit the bill of straight-from-the-grave, bloodsucking ghouls. We must be something else."

He grew quiet. "We don't have to resemble movie-character vampires to qualify, Ellie. We fly, and I don't think you can deny the unique sway of blood over us. I don't know how the whole 'flash' thing fits in, but really, what else could we be?"

I had no idea, but from Michael's tone, I could tell he didn't want an argument. I kept quiet. I didn't want to taint the magic of the night with the questions about our nature.

His tone softened, and he squeezed me tight. "Anyway, what does it matter? We have each other, and we're the same. Whatever we are." He gave me a mischievous smile. "Even if I still think we're vampires."

In a way, he was right about it not mattering. Soon enough, we'd have to figure out who—or what—we were. So I relaxed into his arms and let my questions rest. For the moment, I allowed myself to just be, whatever I was—with Michael.

Seventeen

I did transform, though the change did not happen overnight. I discovered that, as I acknowledged the existence of my powers to myself, they grew. A new Ellie struggled to come into being sooner than I imagined possible, one that liked the gifts—the differences—that surged beneath the surface. Almost as if she'd been sleeping for a long, long time and had finally awakened.

At first, I managed to keep the two parts—the powerful nighttime self and the ordinary daytime self—completely separate. But then, my nocturnal side began to creep into the day. As I walked down the school hallways, I felt the power race through my fingertips, and a war began to simmer beneath my seemingly normal surface. I knew I had the ability to see the other kids' true identities and darkest secrets—and I itched to do it. Sometimes, it was all I could do to stop myself from reaching out and touching them, even helping them with their secret problems. Was this compulsion part of whatever I was? It was heady, tempting stuff, and I could barely maintain the facade of the old Ellie.

But I had to keep up appearances; otherwise my dual existence would unravel. This meant stopping for coffee with Ruth and having dinner with my parents, as well as paying attention in class and laboring at my homework. As if nothing had changed. Even though I'd tried to keep my normal routines with Ruth—lunch every day, coffee after school on Fridays, even the Odeon—I knew that the veneer wasn't without cracks. I had a whole life with Michael from midnight to five A.M.—not to mention a whole new secret self—and it made regular activities challenging, to say the least. The role-playing made me feel exhausted and conflicted, particularly around Ruth, with whom I'd vowed to share everything.

One morning, after the ongoing torture of Miss Taunton's class, I stopped in the bathroom on the way to calculus. I needed a minute alone to compose myself.

The bathroom looked empty, but as I washed my hands, I thought I heard an odd noise in the back stall. I turned off the water and waited a minute in silence. The total quiet made me doubt myself. I reached for the faucet to finish cleaning up when I heard a stifled sob.

The girl must have thought the stillness signaled my departure, because the stall door slammed open a second later. Out stepped Piper.

I was so shocked to see a pretty, popular girl crying in the school bathroom stall that I froze. Girls like her never showed weakness, at least not during school. When I finally regained my composure, my compassion, and my manners, I asked, "Are you all right, Piper? Here, let me get you something." I rushed over to the paper towel dispenser. Although Piper and I usually ignored each other in school, we had long maintained a civil, albeit secretive, relationship outside of it.

The typical school Piper resurfaced, and she waved her hand dismissively as if I was her servant. "No, no, Ellie. I'm fine. I've just got something in my eye." I hated it when she reverted to her school behavior, as if I didn't know the other side of her.

I caught a glimpse of her in the bathroom mirror as she patted down her face. A wayward eyelash could not possibly explain her swollen eyes, tear-streaked cheeks, and blotchy nose. If it had been any of her jerky friends, for whom I couldn't muster up a shred of sympathy, I might have laughed at the lame excuse. But I couldn't mock Piper under the circumstances.

"Come on, Piper. You look really upset. Can I do anything to help?"

She stopped her ministrations and gave me a cold, hard stare. "Yes, you can."

"What can I do?"

"Don't tell anyone that you saw me in here crying." And with that command, she pulled out her makeup bag and started to powder her mottled face.

"Tell who? Ruth?"

"I don't care about Ruth." She waved her hand dismissively. Then her voice changed. "But everyone knows that you and Michael Chase are seeing each other. Don't tell him, okay? He knows a lot of the guys. He could really spread it around if he wanted to."

Piper wouldn't care so much if her friends weren't the source of her tears. I was really curious to know what they did to cow the indomitable Piper.

"Don't worry, Piper. I won't mention it to him or anyone else," I lied. Then I handed her the paper towel I'd grabbed, brushing my fingers up against her hand ever so slightly.

The flash hit me hard. I saw Missy just inches from Piper's face, as if I were Piper. Missy was screaming, her expression venomous. I felt Piper cringe in terror as words lashed out of Missy's mouth like a whip.

"Who do you think you are? How dare you mess with

my plans?" Missy shrieked.

"I'm sorry, Missy. I just think that we might be going too far," Piper said. I sensed that it was really tough for Piper to disagree with Missy, but for once, she felt compelled to take a stand.

Piper shuddered as the malicious look faded from Missy's face, only to be replaced by a smile. It seemed that she feared a grinning Missy more than an overtly malevolent one. "Really? Too far?" Missy asked, mocking her.

"Yes," Piper said, although her voice was weakening.

Missy kept smiling and started to circle Piper slowly, like a hawk about to attack its prey. There was someone else standing behind Missy, but I couldn't see who it was. Because Piper didn't dare take her eyes off Missy. "It suddenly occurred to me that you might be a better subject for my plan than the person I originally picked," Missy finally said.

"Me?" Piper had to work hard to keep her voice steady.

Missy stopped circling and got right into Piper's face. "Yes, you."

I could feel Piper's heart race. "I was wrong, Missy. Your plan is perfect just the way it is. Let's go ahead with it."

Missy's threatening smile became a triumphant one, and she beamed it at Piper and the shadowy figure behind her. "I knew you'd see reason. We'll start tonight."

Piper stared down at the floor, feeling sick and scared. Even though she didn't look up, she could see Missy rejoin the person at the back and walk with him—I could tell it was a him from his shoes—toward the door. As the mystery guy passed Piper, he reached out and ran a finger along her shoulder. I felt Piper shudder with a strange mix of revulsion and desire.

The image faded, and I returned to the bathroom. I was still standing there with my hand outstretched, having just given Piper the paper towel. Only a second had passed, but it felt like hours. We turned our attention to the mirror, standing next to each as if nothing had happened. Just two girls fixing their hair and makeup. It was surreal.

I watched Piper check me out. "You look good, Ellie."

"Thanks," I said and glanced at myself in the mirror. Instead of my typical jeans and T-shirt, I was wearing a printed top and skinny black pants that somehow worked. Michael's encouragement and my own increasing self-confidence had emboldened me to try out some new looks. I still felt awkward, but I liked Michael's reaction. The clothes seemed to suit my new self a little better.

"Michael has changed you for the better."

I smiled. He had affected me, but not in the way she imagined. "I'll be sure to tell him." I zipped up my bag, ready to leave the bathroom.

Piper shot me one last imploring look before I left. The mask slipped, and she showed her neighbor face, rather than her school face. "Please, Ellie, don't tell anyone what you saw in here."

If she only knew what I saw.

Eighteen

The flash plagued me all day at school, even driving out my usual temptations to read the other kids. By the time my painful after-school meeting with Miss Taunton was over, I practically ran to the Daily Grind to meet Ruth. I figured that she might have heard something about Missy and Piper's plan, and I itched to learn more.

In my haste to open the coffee shop door, I nearly crashed into the back of a man who walked in just before me. As I started to apologize, he turned around to face me. He had blond hair and bright blue eyes, and wore a sweater and jeans. But his age confused me; he wasn't an old man exactly, but he seemed a lot older than the teen-age guys who hung around the Daily Grind. Maybe he was a college student. I couldn't deny that the man, or kid, was handsome, but there was an unsettling quality to his attractiveness. I found him appealing and repellent at once. Particularly when he smiled a strange, bemused smile at me in forgiveness for my clumsiness.

Unnerved, I eked out one more "I'm sorry," and raced over to the table where Ruth waited with my latte. I was worried that she'd notice how flustered I was, but she was utterly preoccupied by the upcoming Fall Dance. Jamie from English had asked her—the Jamie I'd seen Ruth fantasize about in that one flash—so the four of us were going together. I sipped my coffee and listened to Ruth chat away, while I waited for my heart to stop racing from my peculiar little encounter.

"So are we going shopping for your dress this weekend?" I asked, grateful for the coffee. I needed the caffeine; the late nights were taking their toll.

She smiled. "Yes, I can't wait. I've been looking through magazines for ideas. I even found something perfect for you."

"Oh?"

"Yeah, it's in this really cool blue color that'll look great with your eyes."

I hadn't wanted to tell Ruth, but I already had my dress. One day after school, Michael and I passed the only really nice boutique in Tillinghast, and he practically dragged me in. He stood outside the dressing room while I tried on six dresses he picked out. I refused to leave the room to let him see me in any of the first five. But when I slipped on the last one, a red strapless silk dress with shirring around the bodice, I couldn't stay in that room. I looked and felt so different, but I wasn't certain. I needed Michael to be my reflection.

When I stepped out into the store, Michael's reaction told me it was the one. As I stood in front of the full-length mirror, he came up behind me, put his hands on my shoulders, and whispered. Sitting there at the table with Ruth, I almost shivered thinking about what he said: "You look as beautiful as when you fly."

Ruth paused for a second, and I figured I had my opening to ask about the flash from Piper. Discreetly, of course.

"Have you heard any gossip about Missy or Piper lately?" I figured if anyone knew about the plan outside the inner circle, it would be Ruth. Her unassuming exterior masked an insatiably curious mind and provided the perfect cover for some adept eavesdropping. I knew I could have just touched her to see if she had any information, but I'd learned that it was impossible to act normally around her if I read her thoughts. So I continued to abstain from reading Ruth.

"No, other than the normal junk about boyfriends and parties. Why do you ask? You usually don't care."

"I overheard something about some plan of theirs. It sounded like it might be nasty."

"A plan from those two? Who did you hear talking?"

How could I explain my source? For about the millionth time, I felt guilty about keeping secrets from her. I scrounged around for an explanation, and said something close to the truth: "I was in the bathroom, and I heard two girls talking by the sink."

"Did you recognize the voices at all?"

"It sounded a little bit like Piper and Missy."

"I'll keep my ears open."

"Thanks." I didn't know why I cared. After all, Piper's problems were her own, and she'd never reach out to help me. But since I'd acknowledged my gifts, I'd been experiencing this overwhelming Good Samaritan impulse, and the flash I experienced with Piper left me with the desire to swoop in and help out this unknown victim.

"Although seriously, Ellie, I don't think I'll hear anything. Piper and Missy don't have the brains."

I was about to disagree—maybe Piper and Missy couldn't take the heat of an AP class but they were no dummies in the scheming department—when she blurted out, "Is everything all right, Ellie?"

It was the question I'd been dreading. I really hated to lie to Ruth outright. "Yeah, of course. Why do you ask?"

"You seem so distant sometimes."

"I'm really sorry, Ruth. It's just that—" I started to trot out the excuse I'd prepared just for this occasion, when

Ruth's attention drifted off. She was staring at something or someone behind me. Wondering if she was trying to demonstrate just how inattentive I'd become, I twisted around to follow her gaze.

She openly gawked at a guy sitting in the red club chair in the corner of the coffee shop—the guy I'd nearly crashed into when I walked in. From afar, he appeared even cuter, since the distance muted the whole disconcerting quality. He held a cup of coffee and a newspaper like most of the other people in the store, but somehow they looked like movie props and his clothes looked like a costume. Because he was far too good-looking for Tillinghast.

I spun back to Ruth to discuss him, and realized that she would disagree with any observation of him I might have. He mesmerized her. I literally had to snap my fingers and call her name before she tore her eyes away from him. And when she did, I was thankful he'd visited our coffee shop rather than the Starbucks across the street, whatever lingering eeriness I felt about him. Because the very presence of this strange man made Ruth forget all about her question.

Nineteen

That night, Michael and I lay in our field, spent from flying along the coast. My head rested on Michael's arm as we stared up at the night sky. The grass was springy and soft after a light afternoon rain, almost as if we'd spread out a blanket. I felt so peaceful that I didn't want to bring up my flash with Piper. But I couldn't stop thinking about it.

"What's wrong, Ellie?"

Clearly my attempts to act normal weren't working.

"I had this really weird flash today, and I just can't shake it."

"What was it?"

I told him every detail of the vision I could remember. The exchange between Missy and Piper. The references to a plan. The strange guy lurking in the background. The fear that Piper experienced.

Michael listened carefully, and then asked, "Of all the

flashes you've had, why should this one affect you so much?"

His reaction disappointed me; he didn't seem particularly moved. Maybe I expected too much. Maybe I expected him to feel everything I felt. We were alike in so many ways.

"I don't know. But I feel like I need to find out more and do something."

He twirled a strand of my black hair in his fingers and then sighed. "Why, Ellie? They're such jerks. You don't need to rescue Piper from anything."

"It's not Piper that I plan on rescuing. It's the victim."

"That's very noble, Ellie. But we're not superheroes."

I sat up. Michael had pulled me away kicking and screaming from my somewhat happy oblivion into this new existence. He basically made me acknowledge and embrace these "differences" of ours—and now he wanted me to ignore the impulse to help that came along with some of the flashes. This one especially. "No, Michael, we're not superheroes. But we're something more than regular humans."

"I know. But I don't see why that obliges us to fly in and clean up whatever mess Missy and Piper are making."

"Michael, I can't ignore this compulsion to get involved. Don't you ever feel it?" I had just assumed that he did. I'd never felt the urge to assist so intensely before, but I did experience it from time to time when a classmate transmitted a particularly troubling image to me.

"A little, I guess."

"Ever since we started"—I gestured around the field—"all this, I've been getting the strong feeling that we should use our gifts for something other than our own entertainment. Like helping the people whose minds we read. Do you ever get that sensation?"

He paused for a second. I saw his hand reaching out to stroke mine, but I drew back a little. I didn't want this conversation to be tainted by his touch; I was just too susceptible. "I guess I've been so wrapped up in you that I haven't let those thoughts get much play," he said.

For all my efforts to keep a physical distance, I felt like melting. Here was the guy of my dreams telling me that I so distracted him he couldn't see straight. How could I be irritated with him? Especially since I felt the same way.

Still, I wanted him on board with me. Not just about this Piper and Missy incident. I wanted him to feel what I felt. And given all my parents' training about helping out mankind, I was more than a little disappointed that he didn't.

"If you did think about this idea—that we have some kind of obligation to others because of our differences—what would you think?"

Even in the darkness of the moonless night, I could see

Michael smile at me. "I've never heard of do-gooder vampires," he joked, to which I rolled my eyes. "What would I
think?" he continued. "I'll tell you what I do think. I think
that I'm lucky that you are sharing this experience with
me. And I think that I'll help you. Because, even though I
don't care about Piper and Missy, I care about you."

I curled into the crook of his arm, and whispered,
"Thank you."

We talked for a moment about a game plan for gathering information and then Michael whispered, "Ellie?"

"Yes?" I answered. His tone was so silky and inviting
that I figured he was going to kiss me. He usually did at the
end of the night. But I was always careful to stop it there;
those first experiences kissing him really shook me up, and
I didn't want to lose control.

His lips tickled my cheek, and his sweet breath warmed
me. I turned my face toward his, ready.

In that same honeyed voice, he said, "You know if we
used their blood, we could find out nearly anything."

"Michael," I said in frustration. He knew how I felt
about the whole blood thing. And anyway, I wanted a kiss,
not another argument on this topic.

"Come on, Ellie. It'd be a chance to try out its power."

Other than those first few, unplanned occasions, I hadn't
tried Michael's blood. Or let him try mine. I remembered

the addictive headiness of its taste all too well, and it scared me. I was afraid that, once I started, I wouldn't be able to turn back. But I couldn't tell Michael that.

"No."

"It would be for a good cause," he said suggestively, as he traced his finger up and down my arm.

"You'll try anything to persuade me, won't you?"

He just smiled, unable to deny it.

"Let's see if we can't find another way," I said and kissed his neck very lightly.

"Now who's being persuasive?" he said, his voice growing thick.

It was my turn to smile.

He said, "All right, we'll try it your way first. But promise you'll just consider—"

"I promise."

I kissed him hard. I was so relieved and happy that he was on my side for the Piper thing, I let my guard down. Within seconds, we were wrapped in each other's arms. I felt his tongue on mine, and I surrendered to the feeling of it. He must have sensed that I wouldn't fight him, because I soon felt a tiny cut on my tongue and tasted the blood. His and mine. Together.

The sensation was pure pleasure, unlike anything I'd ever experienced. I closed my eyes and let the bliss wash

over me. Until a flash—more like a vision than a memory—
came. The light was blinding; I squinted in my mind's eye.
As my vision adjusted, I saw Michael and me standing on a
pristine beach of white sand, arcs of light at our backs. We
looked so beautiful, so serene. And then I noticed something really peculiar. Emblazoned across our chests were
letters, written in light. I struggled to read them, but the
characters were in an unfamiliar language.

I could have lingered in the moment, but I felt Michael's
tongue graze over my teeth again and I knew he was
searching for more blood. I awakened from the image,
understanding that, if we continued this practice of blood
sharing, we would never, ever stop.

I pushed Michael off me and sat up. I struggled to speak.
"Do you understand why we can't do this with anyone else?
Why we shouldn't even do this with each other? Do you
see how you can't stop hunting for blood once you start?"

"I do." His breath was belabored.

"Promise me, Michael, you'll never taste anyone's blood
but mine."

He stared into my eyes, his chest still heaving but his
gaze steady. "I promise."

TWENTY

Michael and I had agreed to divide and conquer Missy's clique. I took Piper for obvious reasons and Missy out of guilt, since I'd instigated this whole thing. In exchange for my handling of the heavy hitters, Michael took the remaining six group members—Hallie, Kristen, Elizabeth, Samantha, Jennifer, and Shadley. Soon we unleashed ourselves on the unsuspecting Tillinghast Upper High School.

Or so we believed. We had this fantasy of sauntering in, touching them, and gathering up all their secrets. Not so, when we had specific secrets we wanted to gather.

The stars had to be perfectly aligned to learn the tiniest detail. First, we had to actually make physical contact. Then, the person had to be thinking about the scheme at the exact moment we touched them. Finally, the flash—if we were lucky enough to get the one we sought—had to make sense. We had learned that people's thoughts weren't linear, but often so disjointed and jumbled that we couldn't understand the image.

But the most difficult part was touching them. How could we brush up against them and make it seem accidental—instead of looking like some kind of a pervert? Plus I faced an additional hurdle. Usually, I avoided Missy and Piper at all costs. But now I had to place myself in their path in a seemingly natural way—and then find a way to touch one or both of the school's most unapproachable junior girls. It wasn't easy, particularly since they seemed to have abandoned their efforts to woo me.

I lingered at my locker, hoping to run into them. To no avail. I memorized their class schedules, and I shifted my route so I could bump into them. Without success. I forced poor Ruth to have coffee at the Starbucks instead of the Daily Grind because that's where they hung out. No sightings. After all these weeks of trying unsuccessfully to avoid them, suddenly I couldn't cross their paths to save my life.

Michael's efforts were stymied as well. While he had more luck making physical contact with the group's minor members than I did—no surprise given that he was a cute senior guy—he couldn't wrangle any relevant images from their minds. Whether the reason stemmed from their ignorance about the plan or the fact they weren't thinking about it when Michael made contact, we didn't know.

But he loved to torment me a little with the description of romantic images of himself he extracted from some of their minds.

In desperation, I thought maybe I'd try the next-door neighbor gambit. I hoped beyond all hope that the friendlier version of Piper who appeared once we left school might be more amenable to my efforts. But, day after day, a solid opportunity eluded me.

One afternoon, while my mom was making cookies, I spotted my chance. Much to her astonishment, I offered to drop off a dozen at the Faireses as a "friendly" gesture. Both of Piper's parents worked pretty long days—her mom was a secretary at the university and her dad was an associate professor of political science—and I guessed they'd still be at work. I'd seen Piper's car in the driveway, so I figured that I might have a few minutes alone with her.

I had no fixed game plan, but I had to try. Balancing the tinfoil-wrapped plate on my hip, I walked the short distance between our two houses. Then I lifted the ancient door knocker and let it bang down with a clang. As I'd hoped, within a few seconds, Piper opened the door.

Her mouth was wide in surprise at the sight of me on her doorstep. Since I came bearing gifts, she had no choice but to invite me in. As she held the door open for me, I grazed my finger against her forearm. All I got was a faint image—as weak as milky tea—of her struggling over an English paper on Shakespeare. I must have interrupted her homework.

Piper ushered me into the kitchen, thanked me, and pointed to an open spot on the counter to lay the cookies. Her neighborly duty done, she pivoted and started to walk back toward the door. I was about to be discharged like a servant; apparently, friendly Piper was not going to make an appearance. Not readily, anyway.

I had to get her thinking about the plan and make contact. Fast.

"So, are you doing all right?" I asked, all concern and empathy.

"Yeah, why wouldn't I be?" Piper had a quizzical expression on her face, but it looked forced. She knew what I was talking about.

"You know, the bathroom."

"Oh, that," she said with a wave of her hand. "That was nothing, like I said."

Here was my chance.

"Well, if you ever need anyone to talk to . . ." I reached out and touched her shoulder.

I got a strong flash. The vision showed her and Missy in the school library, transfixed by Piper's laptop. They were sitting so close, I could actually smell the coffee on Missy's breath. Looking through Piper's eyes, I saw an open Facebook page.

Missy was barking orders at Piper. "Hurry up, Piper. I've got to meet Zeke at the Till in ten minutes." The Till was a bar frequented primarily by university students, and had a pretty strict carding policy. How did Missy think she would get in there?

Piper typed furiously in response, but didn't look up. Although, I could feel her heart race and her stomach churn at the mention of Zeke. Who was he? I couldn't think of a single Tillinghast teenager named Zeke. Maybe he was a University student.

As Piper typed, I looked closer at the screen; she and Missy were creating a new user profile. This struck me as odd given that both girls had been active on Facebook forever. Just as I tried to make out the user name, the image faded. I returned to Piper's kitchen.

Piper shook off my hand. "Ellie, I don't need your help." Then she marched off to the front door.

I followed in her wake with a private smile. I didn't care if she dismissed me, because I finally had something to go on.

TWENTY-ONE

I was wrong. The more Michael and I mulled over the flash I'd gotten from Piper, the less excited we became. On closer analysis, the flash didn't really shed much light on the scheme—beyond the Facebook element—or the intended victim. On balance, we were left with more questions than answers.

Even though I hated to admit it, we were both getting a little frustrated and burned-out from our little investigation. So when Michael suggested—in the nicest way possible—that we leave off our "research" for the week before the fall dance, I told him I'd seriously consider it. After he mentioned I was looking worn-out, I agreed to take a break; I wanted to look good for the dance, as he well knew. But I found it hard to put the whole thing out of my mind.

I tried to let the dance distract me. Once Ruth finally

forgave me for buying my dress without her—after I pointed out that it left me more time to dedicate to her search—we spent hours at the mall. She tried on gowns in every shade imaginable—from black to pale green to lavender to chocolate brown—and finally settled on a pale pink dress that looked surprisingly perfect with her reddish hair. The big hurdle over, she then turned her attention to the smaller details like our hair, makeup, shoes, and even nails, not that she thought of these finer points as minor. We pored over countless magazines and visited every Tillinghast makeup counter and shoe store until we found the perfect accessories. Happily, I let her sweep me up in all things dance, relishing feeling like a normal teenager for a change.

We made plans to have everyone meet at my house just before the dance. Everyone included not just me, Ruth, Michael, and Jamie, but the parents as well. Ruth didn't feel comfortable having Jamie pick her up at her house with just her dad around. And anyway, Ruth's dad and my parents were close. Once my parents and Ruth's dad were going to be on the scene, we felt like we had to include the guys' parents too. I never thought the guys would actually ask them. But surprisingly, they did.

Friday night before the dance everything was in place. I

had my dress, shoes, purse, and makeup lined up and ready to go, even though we had hours to get ready on Saturday. I finished my homework that afternoon, so I wouldn't have to think about it Saturday and Sunday. I'd even begged off flying with Michael; I told him that I needed at least one night of uninterrupted sleep to look perfect for the dance. He begrudgingly agreed.

But I couldn't sleep. I was restless, though I couldn't say exactly why. Thoughts of Missy and Piper crept into my consciousness, but they weren't the sole source of my agitation. Anxiety about my powers and what they meant crossed my mind from time to time, yet I'd really let go of my worries over the past week and enjoyed myself. So, why couldn't I sleep? Had I grown used to staying awake all night? Was it just typical pre-dance jitters that average teenage girls experienced? I didn't know.

The minutes ticked by, a half hour, an hour, two hours. I grew madder and madder at myself. I should've just gone flying with Michael; it always tired me out. Finally, at the three-hour mark, I threw off my quilt and sheets and padded over to the computer. I had to do something other than lie there in my bed.

I stared at my Google homepage. Before I knew it, my fingers were racing across the keypad. I looked up and saw the name "Professor Raymond McMaster" typed into the previously blank search box. Where had that come from?

I really hadn't given him much of a thought since that humiliating day in Miss Taunton's class. Or so I thought. My subconscious must have been working on overdrive. The truth was, I didn't feel like a vampire. I always imagined vampires as cold-hearted, or no-hearted. The feelings I felt were . . . big, warm, inclusive. I needed an expert to help me sort this out. I clicked onto the Harvard University webpage and read Professor McMaster's résumé. Under-grad and grad work done at Harvard, followed by a post-grad stint at Oxford. He did an assistant professorship at Stanford, after which he took on his current tenured role back at his alma mater. Impressive. Especially for a Dracula expert.

Scanning down the bio, I saw a list of his published papers. They weren't all about vampires; some of them focused on other "supernatural folklores and mythologies." But vampires certainly seemed to be his specialty. I clicked on one paper that looked particularly interesting: "Multicultural Origins of the Vampire Legend."

I clicked open the paper. The very first words made me shiver unpleasantly. Professor McMaster might not serve as the ally I'd been hoping for, to convince Michael that we were not vampires.

> *Vampires walk among us. Whether the Scottish bao-bhan sith, the Indian baital, the Chinese jiang shi, the Croatian kosci, the Romanian moroi, or the Mexican tlahuelpuchi, every society and every culture harbors vampires. The question is not whether vampires exist—in our collective subconscious or on our streets—but in what form and why.*

Page after page, Professor McMaster's thesis—all around the notion that vampires must be real, given their presence in every civilization—enthralled me. And chilled me. This wasn't some kook spouting off crazy conspiracy theories on the internet, but a respected scholar at Harvard University, of all places.

But, Professor McMaster saved the real zinger—to my mind, anyway—for the last paragraph.

> *This survey makes clear that, although each society's vampires take different forms, they share two unsettling characteristics: an inhuman ability to transport themselves, and a fascination with blood. But while interesting,*

the precise form and nature of a culture's vampires ulti-
mately is of no import to the vampires' purpose. Wherever
they might be found, whatever form they purport to take,
all vampires embody our darkest and most primeval fears
of the unknown and serve as the key to the mystery of
what, if anything, comes after death.

Suddenly, Michael's vampire theory seemed all too possible.

Twenty-two

By morning, I had no time to think about Professor McMaster, vampires, Missy, Piper, or anything other than the fall dance. Ruth arrived at eight A.M. with as many bags as my parents and I took with us on our summer trips and a computer-generated timetable of our appointments and activities. I was never so happy to see Ruth; I didn't want to be alone with my thoughts for company.

All day long, Ruth swept me up in a tidal wave of manicure and pedicure appointments and professional makeup applications. I drew the line at having my hair done by her stylist—no one could ever make sense of my thick, pin-straight hair, not even me—but I watched as Ruth had her hair pinned into a complicated style that really suited her. I thought my parents would balk at all the overt displays of frivolity and materialism, but they didn't. They seemed relieved to have a normal sixteen-year-old daughter getting ready for a dance. I found it a relief to play the part, rather than wallow in the reality that I was some freak of nature, like one of the creatures described by Professor McMaster.

"Ruth, Ellie! Come down, girls. Everyone will be here in a few minutes," my mother yelled up to my bedroom from the base of the staircase.

"Oh my God, it's almost six," Ruth nearly shrieked.

I looked at the clock in disbelief. Had we really been primping and preening for almost ten hours? I guess if I cut out the time we spent getting coffees and lunch as well as the time in transit and gossiping, we had spent more like four hours beautifying ourselves. But still, it was kind of unbelievable.

Ruth and I walked over to my old, stand-alone full-length mirror. Gazing into it, I gave her the once-over first, not quite ready to face my final self.

"You look gorgeous, Ruth," I said and meant it. With her long reddish hair pulled off her face and neck and the pale pink dress setting off her physique, she was transformed into a princess.

She gave me a huge hug and then quickly pulled back to check me out. "Ellie, Michael is going to faint when he sees you. You look so glamorous, like a movie star or something."

Laughing, I stared back at the mirror. I definitely did not look like a movie star, but I looked better. Somehow, the fitted red dress and new makeup enhanced my figure, straight black hair, and blue eyes. Instead of appearing gangly with oddly bright eyes, I looked, well, striking. It felt weird to apply that word to myself even in my private thoughts.

"Girls!" my mother yelled again. That tone meant *hustle*.

Teetering on our heels, we hurried to the top of the staircase. Just as we were about to walk down, we heard a loud knock on the front door.

"Too late," my mother whispered harshly from the bottom stair.

Our momentary delay in front of the mirror cost us. We would now be forced to descend my steep, long staircase with an audience, like a pair of modern-day Scarlett O'Haras. Not exactly the impression I wanted to make on Michael's parents. I'd been kind of hoping to go the nice-girlfriend route, not the drama-queen path.

Glancing at each other first with a mixture of fear and excitement, Ruth and I put on our game faces. We pasted on brave smiles and headed downstairs hand in hand. My dad opened the door about mid-staircase so I couldn't get a good look at our guests until we neared the bottom stair.

When I finally glanced up from the final step, to which I had my eyes glued so I wouldn't fall, there stood Michael, so handsome in a dark blue suit and yellow tie. His green eyes pierced mine, and I didn't need to ask him how I looked. His expression said it all.

In front of everyone, before he even brought me over to his parents, he took me by the hands and kissed me lightly on the lips. Then he strapped an exquisite rose corsage around my wrist; he already knew there was no space for it on the bodice of my dress. He whispered, "It's nowhere near as beautiful as you."

I should've been embarrassed, but I wasn't.

He broke our gaze first, saying, "Mom, Dad, you remember my Ellie."

My Ellie. He knew precisely how to make me melt. I stretched out my hand to a very pretty, chestnut-haired woman who was beginning to gray around the temples. Just like my parents. I'd met his parents twice before— once when they had me over for dinner, and once when we sat together at one of Michael's football games. They were unfailingly pleasant, if a little distant and formal, and somehow we managed to avoid the awkward topic of Guatemala. I still couldn't dredge up an image of Michael from the far reaches of my trip memories.

"Mrs. Chase, it's nice to see you again."

"You too, Ellie. You look absolutely lovely tonight. Michael told me about your dress, but his descriptions didn't do justice to the dress—or you in it."

I blushed, thinking of Michael talking about me to his parents. Trying to ignore the redness of my cheeks, I welcomed his dad next. He was attractive, with an olive complexion and nearly black hair. I kept searching for family resemblances, but blond, fair Michael didn't favor either one of them.

My parents joined our conversation. Out of the corner of my eye, I watched as Ruth, Jamie, and their respective parents made their introductions. The group moved into the living room, and my mom passed around appetizers while my dad poured soft drinks for the kids and wine for the adults.

An hour passed with surprising ease. School and the dance provided ready topics of conversation, and even Ruth's usually recalcitrant dad seemed to relax and open up. Around seven, Michael and Jamie started glancing at their watches and dropping hints that we should leave. The parents acquiesced, but only after they took about a million pictures.

Everyone said their farewells, and Ruth, Jamie, Michael, and I hopped into Michael's car. We had decided on one car. We had no idea what the parking would be like, and in any event, we had agreed to hang out at my house afterward.

Michael was just about to pull out of the driveway, when I called out for him to stop. Unused to carrying a purse, I'd left mine on the kitchen counter.

Michael drove me right to the porch's front steps, and I climbed up them as fast as my spindly heels would allow. Opening the front door, I was relieved that none of the parents were lingering in the front hallway. I wanted to slip in and slip out without the holdup of more chitchat.

Tiptoeing down the back hallway toward the kitchen, I heard my mom and Michael's mom talking. So much for going undetected. But then a rush of water from the kitchen sink sounded. I peeked in and saw our moms' backs as they rinsed off the dishes. Maybe I could slide in and grab my purse unnoticed.

"I still cannot believe that you and Armaros are in Tillinghast," my mom said in a tone that wasn't exactly warm.

"We really had no other choice," Michael's mom said apologetically.

"After we worked so hard to make them forget that they'd ever met—in Guatemala. . . ." My mom's voice trailed off.

"I know. And so successfully with Ellie. Those same techniques didn't work so well with Michael, as you know."

"We did need to have them meet at least once before they come of age, to see how they'd react to one another and to find out what they were capable of together. We needed to take that risk in Guatemala. I just wished they'd fully forgotten each other," my mom said.

The way my mom said it made me wonder whether something awful had happened in Guatemala that they wanted me to forget. If only I could get flashes from my parents or Michael about that trip. I'd tried without success. I kept coming up against that same wall.

My thoughts were interrupted by Michael's mom. "I know, and that's the only reason we've let them spend time together. But it would be so much easier to keep them in the dark until it's time."

"It would have been easier if you'd stayed away from Tillinghast," my mom replied, her voice getting louder and angrier.

"You know that the best way to protect them is to have them in the same location. To keep watch over them."

"You should have contacted us beforehand."

"It didn't seem wise. You know that. Tonight—all of us together in one place—was risk enough." Michael's mom sounded almost repentant.

"Even once the children had found each other of their own accord? You didn't think that you should contact us then?" My mom's voice rose; she was really mad.

"We couldn't take the chance, Hananel. It seemed better to wait and allow their relationship to develop of its own accord. And watch."

Hananel? Who was Hananel? My mom's name was Hannah. And what were they talking about?

My mom was almost screaming. "Watch? Those are rich words coming from a former watcher, whose watching was anything but passive waiting. Just what did you think this passive waiting and watching would gain us?"

"Time, Hananel. I thought the watching would give us time."

My purse dropped to the ground with a clap, and both women pivoted toward me.

"Ellie, honey, I thought you'd gone," my mom said, her voice as sweet as sugar.

I bent down to pick up my purse and brandished it like a sword. I smiled as if I hadn't heard a thing, and said, "Couldn't leave without my purse, could I?" Then, uncertain of what to say or do, I waved good-bye and raced back to the car. The conversation I overheard was bizarre, to say the least, but I wouldn't let it ruin my first dance with Michael.

TWENTY-THREE

The expression on our classmates' faces as we walked into the gym was worth every moment of preparation. The girls mostly gave Ruth and me sidelong glances of appreciation and mild astonishment, but the guys were another story. Some of them openly gaped as we sauntered across the room.

Ruth basked in the attention, and I could tell that Jamie derived a certain vicarious thrill being by her side. As for myself, I experienced a surge of power not unlike the sensation I got when I had a strong flash. And looking at Michael, I saw that he did as well. The feeling helped dispel the nagging voice inside my head about the conversation I'd overheard in the kitchen, which I hadn't dared to mention to Michael yet. I didn't want to ruin our perfectly normal teenage night with a reminder of our strangeness.

We smiled at the other kids as they stared at us, and tried to act casual. The four of us commented on how the dance committee had really transformed the place. Our gym no longer looked like a relic from decades past, but more like an intentionally retro eighties dance club.

All the while, Ruth's voice buzzed like a little bee in my ear as she gave a running commentary on the other girls' dresses. Lexie, she pronounced, looked great in her strapless blue mini, as did Charlotte in her black-and-white lace dress. But, Ruth said, what was Nikki thinking wearing that gold satin full-length gown with a crystal neckline?

I spotted Piper and Missy in a dark corner, almost behind a set of bleachers. The out-of-the-limelight spot seemed odd for the girls; I expected them to hold court front and center, especially at an event like this. And where were their dates? I knew Piper was going with Lucas, but I wondered who Missy's date was. I hadn't seen her with Charlie lately, but I had spotted her walking up the library stairs with that other guy. I guessed that guy was the Zeke mentioned in the flashes, and the figure I'd seen in the shadows.

Maybe Piper and Missy had sequestered themselves in the corner because one or both was mad that they hadn't been named Fall Queen, and maybe that had something to do with their plan. Their former friend Vanessa had somehow managed to rally an overwhelming majority in order to win the votes. I stopped dead in my tracks. Why was I spending even a minute of my night thinking about them, especially when Michael and I had made a pact to take a break from our investigation? I pushed all thoughts of Piper and Missy out of my mind so I could enjoy my night.

One of my favorite songs, Coldplay's "Lost," started to play, and Michael pulled me onto the dance floor. He carved out a place for us in the crowd, and then wrapped his arms tightly around my back. I looked up into his green eyes, bright even in the darkened room. For the millionth time, I thought how lucky I was to have found him.

The music grew louder, and he pressed his body up against mine. I held on to his strong upper arms and rested my head on his shoulder. The tempo of the song picked up, but Michael slowed down. He lifted up my chin and leaned down to kiss me.

His lips felt so soft, so inviting. I kissed him back and savored the gentle touch of his tongue. As he ran his tongue lightly over my teeth, I began to experience a surge of desire for him, unlike anything I'd felt during the many times I'd been physically close to him before. But this was no normal desire to kiss him, or go further. This was different than anything I'd ever felt before. This was bloodlust.

We broke off and stared at each other. Michael felt it too. We had to leave the dance floor before something happened. Something we couldn't control. Something that would freak out everyone around us.

"I'm going to the bathroom to freshen up," I said, for the benefit of anyone nearby who might be listening.

"Do you want me to come with you?" he asked, his voice cracking a bit.

"No, no." The last thing I needed was Michael in close proximity to me. He shot me a concerned look, so I smiled and reassured him. "I'll be fine."

Michael walked me to the gym door nearest the bathrooms. He gave me a kiss on the cheek and then leaned against the wall, as if he needed its support. "I'll wait right here," he said, still breathing a little heavy.

I nodded and opened the door. A little unsteady on my feet—and my heels—I wobbled out into the jarring fluorescent glare of the hall. Blinking in the bright light, I turned right toward the girls' room. A long line of girls— all waiting to jockey for position in front of the mirror, no doubt—snaked out of the door into the hallway. I just couldn't face all that aggressive female energy in my state.

Instead, I turned left, passing by the gym doors. Maybe a little walk would help distance me from the urge. I started down an empty hallway, lined with lockers and classroom doors. Funny how the hall looked so unintimidating and small without all the kids streaming through it. After I cooled down, I turned back toward the gym—and Michael.

Then I heard a whimper from a connecting hallway.

Backing up a few steps, I peeked down the hall. On first glance, it appeared empty. But then I saw a small movement in a darkened doorway, and I heard the whimper again. I hesitated. I really didn't want to deal with someone else's problems tonight of all nights. But the Good Samaritan in me won out over my apprehensions.

Not bothering to soften the click of my heels, I approached the dark niche. The whimper grew louder and became an actual bawl by the time I got there.

"Are you okay?" I said to the girl cowering in the doorway. Her face was buried in her hands, but I could see her upswept auburn hair and her chocolate brown dress. Maybe the poor girl had gotten into a fight with her date.

The girl lowered her hands. At first, all I could see was the welt on her cheek from a hard slap and a long, bloody scratch on her arm, undoubtedly from a fingernail. Only then did I realize that the girl was Piper.

I almost left. Another thankless encounter with Piper wasn't what I needed. And anyway, it was my special night with Michael. But then I smelled a strong metallic odor, and I realized that I couldn't leave, even if I tried. The smell was Piper's blood, welling up from the deep scratch on her arm. It mingled with the distinctive smell of someone else's blood. Maybe the blood of the other person she'd fought with. How I could detect and discern the presence of two distinct blood scents was beyond me.

More than anything in the world, I wanted to touch and taste the blood, and not just because I sought information about her and Missy's scheme. My instinct compelled me to do it. No matter the promise that Michael and I made about not tasting anyone else's blood.

As I reached into my purse for a tissue, I asked her, "Who did this to you?"

"It doesn't matter," she said with a sob.

"Of course it matters, Piper."

Tissue in hand, I leaned forward as if to dab her wound clean. As I did so, I touched some of the blood from her wound with my fingertip. Then I turned away slightly— ostensibly to reach for another tissue from my purse—and licked it.

The blood burned like liquor as it coursed down my throat and made me woozy immediately. Then two separate flashes struck. Their force nearly knocked me off my heels, and I reached for the wall to steady myself. Stronger than any flashes I'd received from anyone but Michael, they told me everything I wanted to know. And much, much more that I didn't want to know.

TWENTY-FOUR

Without a word to Piper, I kicked off my shoes and carried them with me as I ran back down the hall. I didn't have a spare second to make excuses to Piper, and she didn't deserve them. I needed every moment to get to the gym and stop the figurative bloodshed.

The hall seemed to have doubled in size since I walked down it a few short minutes before, like some hazy, frustrating dream. I longed to fly down the hall, but had to rely on my gangly legs to propel me. The slower gait gave me all too much time to think about the malevolent images I'd culled from the blood. And it gave me too much time to think of Vanessa, Missy and Piper's victim.

Why hadn't we thought of Vanessa? This summer, she'd been on the outs with the group for trying to unseat Missy from her veritable throne. Since then, Vanessa had been relegated to the "reject" lunch table, below Missy's notice. Michael and I had believed that Missy had deemed the cafeteria demotion adequate punishment for whatever wrong Vanessa had inflected on Missy. Not so.

The first flash from Piper told me that, just before Vanessa would be crowned Fall Queen, every single Tillinghast junior and senior would receive an email on their cells inviting them to be Vanessa's Facebook friend. The perfectly timed invitation would be irresistible to nearly everyone at the dance, who presumably would accept and be transferred immediately to Vanessa's page. There, via a dummy account, Missy and Piper had posted not only a montage of horrific drunken photos of Vanessa but—worse—entries purportedly from Vanessa that revealed a litany of awful, humiliating secrets about many of Tillinghast's juniors and seniors. It wasn't normal dirt in those entries, but terrible things like cheating and hidden pregnancies and familial meltdowns. The whole plan was designed to disgrace Vanessa and, through her supposed revelation of so many people's closest-kept secrets, make her the object of everyone's hatred. The only redeeming second of the flash was the disgust Piper felt for participating in it. Not that her distaste stopped her, mind you.

But it was the second flash that transmitted a sense of evil so palpable that I felt sick. The flash seemed to come from Missy, the source of the other blood. Through her eyes, I saw her in a tight embrace with some guy. Because she had her head nestled on his shoulder, I couldn't see the guy's face, just the fine black fabric of his suit jacket. But I could hear his voice. In the most enticing whisper imaginable, he told her that she was beautiful and deserved the Fall Queen crown more than anyone in the world. Though his words sounded like innocent flattery, somehow they had spurred Missy on to this plan and made her want to bathe Vanessa in metaphorical blood at the moment of her crowning. I saw—in her soul, it seemed— a desire for wickedness and destruction worse than my worst nightmares.

Finally, finally, I reached the gym door. I pulled it open and ran over to Michael, who was still leaning up against the same spot on the wall. I struggled to speak; it was amazing how running tired me out so quickly, when I could fly for hours with ease. "I know what Missy and Piper are going to do."

Gaping at my disheveled state, he grabbed me by the shoulders. "Are you okay?"

I brushed aside his hands. "I'm fine. Michael, I don't have much time. Have they announced the Fall Queen yet?"

"No, Vanessa and Keith are still standing over there. I

think the crowning ceremony is supposed to start in a few minutes."

Still panting, I said, "Good, I still have time to stop it. Or defuse it, at least."

"Defuse? As in a bomb?" From the terrified look on his face, I saw that he thought—by my unfortunate choice of the word "defuse"—I meant something much worse.

"Don't worry. It's not a literal bomb, but it's still really awful."

I wanted—no, needed—to save Vanessa and all the other kids from the virtual bloodbath about to rain down on them. And there was only one way to do it in the time I had available. To sacrifice myself by naming myself as the creator of the Facebook entries and deem them fiction. To point the finger at anyone else as the architect of this scheme left too much room for denial—and possible belief by the viewers in the horrific stories they'd see on the Facebook page. I couldn't let that happen.

I didn't have enough time to explain my intentions to Michael before the room started buzzing with cell phones containing Facebook invitations from Vanessa. Leaning down, I quickly strapped my shoes back on. I reached into my purse and slid out my brush and lipstick. As Michael stared incredulously, I hurriedly fixed my hair and makeup. If I was going down like a phoenix into the ashes, I wanted to look presentable—even good—doing it.

I gave Michael a kiss, and whispered, "I'm so sorry that I'm about to ruin our night."

Turning toward the stage, I heard him call out, "Ellie, what's going on?"

I could hear the apprehension in his voice, but I couldn't look at him. His concern would only make me hesitate, and I couldn't afford to falter.

Squaring my shoulders and taking a deep breath, I walked to the front of the gym. Out of the corner of my eye, I spotted Vanessa and Keith preparing to go on stage. Ignoring them as best I could, I started up the stairs. A couple of kids and at least one teacher tried to discourage me. But I just smiled and plowed ahead.

Once on stage, I searched around for the mike. The white-knuckled student council president held it tightly in his hand as he reviewed the note cards for his speech. I sidled up to him and said, ever so sweetly, "Can I borrow that for a minute?"

Surprised at the request, he said, "Um, I'm about to make a speech."

Smiling agreeably, I said, "I know. I just have to make a quick announcement first."

"Sure," he said with a smile and handed me the mike.

"Thanks so much. You can have it back in a second, I promise."

Mike in hand, I stared out at the crowd. My self-assurance—real and pretend—left me as I surveyed the nearly two hundred kids on the dance floor. But I couldn't succumb to my fears; I had to move forward. I was moved by a compulsion that was more powerful than anything I had ever felt. Even my desire for Michael.

I cleared my throat and said, "Hi. For those of you who don't know me, I'm Ellie Faneuil."

Even though the kids had stopped dancing, they continued to mill around and talk. They appeared as uninterested and unimpressed with the Fall Queen and King crowning ceremony as Michael. I half-waved and tapped the mike. A loud screech reverberated from the speakers, and suddenly I had everyone's attention.

"I'm sorry to interrupt your night. In a few minutes, you will all receive a Facebook invitation from Vanessa Moore, our Fall Queen. If you accept the invitation, you will be directed to a Facebook page that contains several pictures that seem to be of Vanessa and some posts allegedly by her hand. But the page is complete fiction. The pictures are Photoshopped, and the entries are made up." I paused; the next words stuck in my throat. "I created the entire thing."

In the crowd, I saw Ruth's face staring up at me in

disbelief. The magnitude of my actions hit me, and my voice cracked. "I want to apologize to Vanessa and everyone else named on the Facebook page. Even though I know none of you will ever be able to forgive me."

Before I handed the mike back to a stunned student council president, I glanced out at the crowd. There, at the center, I saw Missy, murderously furious that her plan had been thwarted. At her side stood a guy—a blond, good-looking guy who had to be her date. A guy who had to be the shadowy Zeke from the flashes.

Something about him seemed familiar, and not just from the visions I'd gotten about him. In the split second before I left the stage, I looked at little closer, and realized that he was the guy from the coffee shop. He noticed my stare, and smiled that strange, bemused smile of his. As if he'd expected me to be up there on that stage all along.

I dropped the mike and ran.

TWENTY-FIVE

Over the next few days, darkness seeped into my soul.

Maybe it came from the hatred of me I saw in my classmates' eyes and minds. When I returned from my three-day suspension for my Facebook prank, as it was dubbed by the administration, I'd become the object of loathing for every student at Tillinghast Upper High School. My locker was vandalized, my homework destroyed before it reached the teachers' hands, my face spit upon. God forbid that I accidentally touched someone; the abhorrence seared my fingertips. But I could speak not a word in my own defense: I conceded that right on the gym stage.

Maybe the darkness came from the evil that I'd witnessed in Missy's heart, or the blood I'd sampled from her via Piper. In the flash from her blood, I saw the desire for such unspeakable acts that I couldn't allow myself to revisit the images. It was like becoming a character in one of Hieronymus Bosch's paintings of hell.

I didn't know the source of the darkness. I knew only that the Good Samaritan compulsion all but disappeared the night of the dance. Looking back, I had no idea why I did what I did. Once I'd realized that I had the capacity to spare all those kids all that pain, I just had to take the fall. Was this part of who I was? It certainly didn't sound like the impulse of a vampire. But really, what did it solve, my taking the fall? Although it wouldn't have fixed anything to point the finger at Missy.

Regardless, all that had vanished. I filled the void left in its wake with me and Michael.

Ruth hadn't spoken to me since the dance, and I wasn't sure why. Since I was certain that she must know that I didn't create the Facebook page, I could only guess that she was furious that I'd ruined her dream night. I couldn't even tell her why. Whatever her reason, her abandonment of me made my own submission to the darkness easier. It was one less tie to my old self.

The only ones who didn't detest me outright were Piper and Missy, who were uniform in their disbelief and confusion even though they were no longer in league as friends. Instead of hating me, they seemed to be frightened of me. And with my urge to act charitably gone, I certainly felt no impulse to reach out toward Piper and encourage her better nature.

Only Michael stood by my side, even though part of

him wished that I'd tell the truth about Missy's act. Only he understood what I had done and why. The knowledge brought us closer. So close that there was no longer any room for anyone else.

By day, Michael and I strode down the Tillinghast school hallways impervious to everyone but ourselves; I felt powerful in a way I'd never experienced. By night, we flew through the skies like gods. Like the vampires that I guessed we were. We surrendered to each other. And to the blood.

"Come on," I urged Michael. Where he used to push me along, I now dared him to follow me. The darkness had filled me with a recklessness I'd never before experienced. I now acted with abandon—without concern for anyone other than Michael.

He didn't move.

"Come on," I said again.

"Are you sure there's no one inside?" Michael didn't sound convinced.

"Positive. I can't sense anyone." Ever since I'd submitted to my powers, my skills had grown. I could scan a building or a room to discover how many people were present. With certainty, I knew the charming little townhouse, which dated from the eighteen hundreds, was empty.

Without waiting for Michael's agreement, I slid open the third-floor window and flew inside. Narrowly missing a stack of boxes, I landed hard on the rickety wooden floor. Another thud ensued, and I knew Michael had followed. My eyes adjusted to the pitch-blackness and I saw a clear path to the attic staircase. I took Michael's hand and led him downstairs.

We'd broken into Rose's, the nicest restaurant in town, the one that all the undergrads dragged their moms and dads to on parents' weekend. It was our two-month anniversary, and Michael wanted to celebrate with a really special dinner even though my parents had grounded me indefinitely. He had scouted out the restaurant during the day to crystallize his plan.

After we got to the ground floor, he directed me to a private room that contained a table for two, as well as a fireplace, a few scattered club chairs, and a couch upholstered in ivory damask. He seated me in one of the chairs and lit the silver candelabras at the table's center and on the mantel. After which he disappeared into the kitchen.

Within a few minutes, Michael returned bearing a large waiter's tray. Delicious aromas wafted from the silver-lidded plates on top. With a flourish, he unfolded a linen napkin and laid it in my lap. Then he placed before me a vase brimming with the restaurant's signature variegated red roses. Finally, he brought the two plates to the table. In a grand gesture, he lifted the lids simultaneously, revealing lobster with asparagus and risotto, dishes that he'd ordered earlier that day. My favorite.

Before he sat down, he knelt next to me and whispered in my ear, "Happy anniversary." We tucked into dinner, talking and laughing—even giggling—as if we were any normal couple. But all the while, we knew that it was only playacting. Michael and I were anything but normal.

After we finished the last bites of a molten chocolate cake, I stood up and stretched out my hand to Michael. He rose, and I led him to the couch facing the fireplace. We hadn't dared light a fire—the chimney smoke would be a giveaway—but we had no need. We could see each other well enough in the dim candlelight; we were used to much less light.

I lay down on the couch and motioned for him to join me. Lowering himself down, he molded his body to mine. Our lips rested up against each other, and for a long moment, we just breathed each other's breath. Through his breath, I experienced every aspect of his day as if I'd been with him the entire time. He did the same. We had no need for words.

Then I kissed him. At first, the sensation was simple, pure pleasure. My lips, his lips, our lips, our tongues. In time, the bloodlust began to build, the same urge we first experienced at the fateful Fall Dance. But we no longer fought it. We yielded to its power.

I ran my tongue along his teeth at the same moment he ran his tongue against mine. Tiny droplets emerged on the tips of our tongue, and our blood mingled. Intense waves of physical delight washed over us. Then, like a slow burn that becomes more intense over time, the images came. I saw Michael and myself with wide swaths of light at our backs and letters of light emblazoned on our chests. I saw us flying through places and times I could not identify or comprehend. I saw us battling and helping and fighting and saving. Much as I didn't understand who or what we were, I didn't comprehend many of the images; indeed most of them seemed vaguely futuristic. Yet I reveled in them.

The visions and the pleasure slowly receded. I lay in Michael's arms, peaceful and content; we never discussed the images, and we rarely talked about our natures. But I knew that, from the instant I awoke until nightfall of the next day, I would wait for this moment. I lived in—and for—it. As did Michael. We had become addicted to each other's blood.

Twenty-six

The next night, I stared at the clock. The hands seemed frozen at 11:50. I prayed and prayed for them to move. I desperately wanted that minute hand to hit the eleven and the twelve. Only then, only at midnight, could I rise from my bed and fly out to meet Michael. I didn't think I could hold off the craving—for Michael and the blood—a minute past twelve.

My countdown had started as soon as I woke up that morning. Every day progressed that way now. As I got ready for school, as I sat in class, as I walked alone down the hallways trying hard to ignore the hateful stares, as I sat at dinner with my parents, I thought about my upcoming night with Michael. Knowing that the sweet release was only hours away made the daytime misery of school bearable.

The clock's hands finally joined at the twelve. Midnight. I wanted to leap from my bed, but instead I peeled back my

quilt quietly, careful not to rustle the sheets. After I lowered my feet to the floor, I stuffed the bed with a blanket
and then tiptoed across the notoriously creaky floorboards.
I carefully modulated every step I took and every move I
made to minimize noise; I didn't want to risk awakening
my sleeping parents.

I made it across the floor to my window with only a
modicum of sound. Then I paused to listen for any stirrings
from my parents. The house was silent.

Bit by bit, I opened the window. Even my gentle efforts
caused the ancient window sash to groan. I winced and
forced myself to wait a moment before pushing it up the
rest of the way. Part of me wondered why I cared so much
about my parents catching me. Most of the time I didn't,
which was probably one reason I'd never mentioned to
Michael that conversation between our parents that I had
overheard. My powers had grown such that my mom and
dad couldn't stop me from meeting Michael, no matter
what tactic they tried. Yet, I guessed that enough of the old
Ellie remained to make me protective of my parents. More
specifically, I guessed that I wanted to protect them from
me, from the vampire, or whatever it was, that I'd become.

Kneeling on the window seat, I created an opening
wide enough to slip my body through. I planned on closing
it once I made it into the nighttime air, as nothing would

awaken my parents quicker than a cold blast. I worked my head, arms, and torso through the aperture and was just about to slide my legs through when I felt a hard tug on my ankle. For a second, I thought that my leg had gotten tangled in one of the blankets folded on my window seat. I shook my leg a little, trying to loosen it from the blanket. But the grasp only tightened.

I froze. The blanket felt distinctly like a hand.

Part of me wanted to just kick my leg loose and fly off, but I knew I couldn't. I had to face him or her. Or worse, I suspected, *them*. Terrified, I slowly slid my body back through the window opening. I delayed sliding my head through until the very last second.

Finally, I mustered up the courage to turn around. There my parents sat, looking oddly vulnerable in their pajamas. My dad settled on the window seat—his hands must have been the ones to pull at me—while my mom perched on my bed. Right on top of the blanket I'd stuffed it with, as a matter of fact. We stared at one another in complete silence. I didn't know what to say or do, and they didn't seem to either.

"Just where do you think you are going, Ellspeth?" my dad asked, breaking the silence. His tone sounded hurt, and he was using the formal "Ellspeth."

"Nowhere," I whispered.

"Does this 'nowhere' include meeting Michael?" my mom asked. Her voice bore none of the soft, injured qualities of my dad's. She was furious.

"I don't know what you're talking about." I sounded unconvincing, even to my own ears.

"We may be trusting, Ellspeth, but we're not fools," she said.

I didn't know how to respond. Obviously I was trying to sneak out, although I hoped they hadn't witnessed the flying piece. I had no idea what they knew or for how long they had been aware of my nocturnal activities. Given that I had no desire to educate them about the details if they were blissfully unaware, I kept quiet.

"Ellspeth, allow me to make clear to you what seems very apparent to your mother and me." My dad's tone started to match my mom's—less hurt and more angry.

"All right," I said.

"We have grounded you for that Facebook incident, which mystifies your mother and me. But you still want to see Michael. So you two thought you'd sneak out of your respective houses late at night and rendezvous somewhere. Am I right?"

I wondered whether I should just cop to my father's tale. After all, his theory was pretty close to reality, and it was far less damning than the full truth. Plus, I could feel the need for Michael's blood pulsating through me. Maybe if I just came clean, they would leave me alone, and I could still meet Michael. Even now, Michael was my focus.

As I considered my response, my mom interjected, "Is Michael waiting for you out in the yard?"

"No," I practically shrieked. Michael and I had planned on meeting in town. But I was late, and I couldn't take the chance that he'd come to my house looking for me. And I absolutely couldn't risk my mom peering out the window for him, only to witness him flying by in search of me.

"Do you admit that you made arrangements to meet him somewhere? Just not here?"

"Yes."

My dad shook his head. "Ellspeth, we are so disappointed in you. This behavior is so uncharacteristic for the daughter we've raised and loved." He looked over at my mother, who nodded in encouragement. "We can't help but think that Michael is somehow influencing your actions. For your own protection, we have decided to ban you from seeing Michael."

"No!" I cried out.

"Yes, Ellspeth." My dad's voice was unusually firm. "We will do whatever it takes to keep you from seeing him."

I could not allow my parents to separate me from Michael. I no longer cared about being a dutiful daughter—all I cared about was Michael and the blood. I felt myself getting furious, felt that expansion I first experienced when I lashed out at Missy. My words and my actions were no longer under my control.

I stood up from the window seat, defiant in the face of their attempt at restraints. "You cannot stop me from seeing him."

My mom rose and got right in my face. She looked the way I felt. "Oh, yes, we can."

"You have no idea what I'm capable of."

"Ellspeth, I think your dad and I know exactly what you are capable of."

Placing my hands on my hips, I matched her expression and then smiled smugly at her. "Oh, really? I don't think that's possible." I didn't wait for her response; I headed straight for the window. I had every intention of flying right out of it, into Michael's arms. I didn't care if they saw. I needed to get to Michael, and I would not let them constrain me.

As I lifted the sash once again, I heard her call out, "You think you're a vampire, don't you?"

TWENTY-SEVEN

I spun around and stared at my mom. Her eyes were so certain and knowing, yet contained no judgment of me and no incredulity. She knew who I was, what I was. I wanted more than anything to ask her how she knew, but the words stalled on my lips. How could I ask an unthinkable question?

Overwhelmed and confused, I fell back on the window seat. I must have looked as disoriented and woozy as I felt, because my parents' hands reached out to steady me. Through the miasma of the moment, I heard my dad say, "It's all right, dearest. We'll help you."

"Help?" I asked with a laugh. How could they help me? This wasn't some high school problem to be solved with a pep talk and a pat on the back. It wasn't a dilemma that a few sessions with the local psychiatrist could cure. No, my parents couldn't help me. No one could help me, not even Michael.

I felt my dad's arm slide around my shoulder and pull me tight. "Would it help you to know that you're not a vampire? Would it help you to know that vampires—as you think of them—don't really exist?"

I didn't answer. I couldn't answer. The whole setting and conversation was becoming increasingly surreal. Was I actually sitting here in my bedroom at midnight talking with my parents about why I was not a vampire? Or was I having one of those awful hyper-real nightmares in which you know you are dreaming but you can't wake yourself up?

My dad filled in the deafening silence. "I'm going to tell you a story, Ellie. It's from the Bible—from Genesis, to be exact—so we have to take it with a grain of salt. But this particular story contains a nugget of truth, a very relevant nugget of truth. So I want you to listen carefully, very carefully."

I'd grown used to my dad's random quotations—even tolerated them—but I was in no mood. Anyway, a story from Genesis was an odd choice for my dad, who claimed he loved the messages and tales of the Bible, but couldn't stomach how organized religions used them. "You said you wanted to 'help' me, Dad. How is that supposed to help?"

"Just listen, Ellie." It was an order. Since he was typically more inclined toward polite requests, I nodded.

"In the beginning, for lack of a better term, God sent some of his spiritual intermediaries—we'll call them angels—to mankind. He wanted these angels to protect his newly formed humans, to teach them about His divinity, and to shepherd them to heaven upon their deaths. Instead, these angels became enchanted by mankind. They became enamored of their purity and innocence and, of course, their physical beauty. They were made in God's image, after all. But most of all, the angels became entranced with mankind's thirst for knowledge, about their world and their origin. Because, you see, the angels knew the answers.

"So, succumbing to their own pride in knowing the world's secrets, the angels began to teach human beings all they knew about the earth—the constellations, the signs of the earth, sun, and moon, knowledge of the clouds, the working of metals, the use of coin, and the art of war. In so doing, they fell in love with mankind. They even took human men and women as spouses and produced a unique race of half man and half angel. These beings were called Nephilim.

"From afar, God watched the acts of these angels. And He was mad. These angels had taken His secrets and corrupted His favorite creation, humankind. They had even dared to fall in love with His creation and made a new creation of their own. And what could be more audaciously

Godlike and defiant than that? Creation was reserved for His hands alone.

"God decided that there was only one way to undo the damage caused by these angels. He had to wipe out the now corrupt humans and the half-breed creations, leaving only a select few pure humans. So he whipped up the flood."

My dad said this last word as if it deserved a capital 'F' and as if I knew what he meant. Which I didn't.

So I asked, "The flood?"

"Noah's flood," he said irritably, as if CNN had just reported the deluge. Then he launched back into his story.

"Anyway, even though He allowed these wayward angels to live, God had no intention of letting them go unpunished. He cast them out of heaven permanently and ordered them to remain on earth. To torment them in their new earth-bound existence, He left them with their immortality and their ethereal skills as a reminder of all they'd lost. Except He took away their ability to procreate with humans, of course.

"Many of these angels were furious with God's command, and decided to retaliate. They embraced their new 'fallen' status, and made concerted efforts to turn the remainders of God's pet creation—humankind—away from His light and toward their own refracted illumination. These fallen angels taught humans to worship earthly glamours that they could control and manipulate. In time, humans began to think that the ideals of these angels—even the angels themselves—were divine. Humankind no longer truly feared and worshipped God. Humans worshipped the idols fashioned by these angels—commerce and technology and consumerism and warfare and themselves, of course. And, in turn, the fallen ones captured—sucked away, if you will— humankind's souls.

"But a few of these fallen angels realized their horrible mistake. They decided to try and work their way back into God's grace by living quietly among humans and redirecting man toward His light. This small group assessed the damage that had been done to the earth and humankind by the other fallen ones, and fashioned a plan of redemption. Certain angels decided to address the corruption of the financial sector, others dealt with the rise of materialism, and so on—and you can see the fruits of their labors these days in the news. In addition, every angel in this group, the good group, tried to utilize their natural talents to guide humankind to God at the critical moment—the instant of their deaths. So using their gifts—their powerful sense of an individual's psyche which they derived from touch or blood, their heightened powers of persuasion, and their ability to fly—they reached out to as many dying humans as they could."

I froze. My dad continued talking about these angels, but his voice receded. I could hear only a constant replay of his description of the angels' abilities. Their skills were mine. Was that what I was? A kind of an angel? For some reason, the concept seemed even more foreign than being a vampire. More impudent.

"Gifts?" I interrupted. I needed to better understand who or what I was.

"In the beginning, all of these angels were given certain abilities to assist them in their work of shepherding souls to God's light. They were endowed with the gift of flight, so they could quickly reach the sides of dying humans to help them before it was too late. The angels were able to see into humans' minds and hearts, so they could understand how they might assist the humans in shedding their worldly cares and choosing a higher plane. They gained this insight by touching the human or—more powerfully—by tasting their blood, their life force. And the angels bore strong powers of persuasion, to better influence the humans' final decisions. The angels were supposed to use these gifts for their intended purposes only—to guide souls to God."

A thought occurred to me. What if you didn't use your powers for their intended objectives, for good? What if you started using them only for your own selfish purposes, like

I had with Michael lately? Could that explain why I'd felt so dark recently? Why I'd sort of lost that compulsion to help others? All these questions assumed that I was an angel, of course. I asked my dad, "What if angels used their gifts for their own purposes?"

My dad paused before answering. I could tell my question kind of disturbed him. "That is precisely what these angels did at first, when they were sent to guard mankind. After all, even angels have free will, the capacity to choose darkness over light. That is why they were cast out. Once these angels were cast out and became fallen, they fully submitted their powers into the service of their own desires. Then the darkness—the urge to serve self rather than something higher—took hold. And that hold was—is—very, very hard to break, nearly like an addiction."

Before continuing, he sort of shivered. Then he pulled himself together and said, "Over the centuries, people in every culture, every society, began to take notice of these angels—especially the fallen angels trying for redemption. Remember, these angels striving for salvation were trying to bring souls to God at the moment of death. People occasionally saw them in that instant, and attributed to them the deaths they witnessed. People started to fear these angels. Who could blame them? Sometimes, the people watched the beings draw close to the dying and whisper in their ears. Other times, they saw the creatures touch their loved ones as they took their last breaths. And in rare occasions, they observed an exchange of blood between the dying human and the being. Of course, the people believed that the beings were causing the deaths—rather than facilitating the afterlife journeys of their loved ones. People created entire legends around these beings. The myths differed from culture to culture, from age to age. But the core always remained the same, and it gave birth to the legend. The legend of the vampire.

"And you can see how that legend was not too far off the mark with certain of the fallen angels, the ones who continued to serve themselves and reject the light. For they used their gifts to suck away humans' souls and create a civilization that worshipped them, instead of God."

My dad paused, and in the quiet, I couldn't help but think that this last bit sounded a lot like the musings of Professor McMaster. Since when was my biologist dad a vampire scholar? Or a biblical scholar, for that matter? I looked over at him and noticed that, during the course of his long talk, his handsome face had grown craggy. He suddenly looked so sad and so old that I couldn't possibly challenge him.

He reached out to caress my cheek. "So my lovely daughter, you cannot possibly be a vampire, because there are no vampires. Only fallen angels. Good and bad."

"How do you know all this?" I finally asked, one among the many questions I'd amassed.

Before answering, he looked over at my mom, who'd remained still and silent during the whole of his monologue. She nodded her head once, and he turned back to me.

"Because humans once called me and your mother vampires."

Twenty-eight

No way. My parents were perfectly normal, perfectly terrestrial. No way were they angels, or vampires, or anything else that whiffed of the otherworld. The very notion of my mom and dad as unearthly beings was ridiculous.

In fact, all of this suddenly felt laughable. It was too much, and I could feel the hysteria bubbling up in me. Tears streamed down my face. My stomach ached from the force of my laughter. When I realized that my parents weren't joining in, the hilarity subsided a little bit. But then I looked over at them, somber and respectable and silent in their flannel nightgown and pajamas and robes, and the whole concept of them flying and divining thoughts seemed so hysterically ridiculous that the laughter took hold again.

Finally, I calmed down enough to ask, "You two? Angels?"

"Yes," my dad said quietly. Almost apologetically.

"So, we're like a family of angels? Are you two the good

kind or the fallen ones?" I said with a giggle.

"We were fallen. But now we are trying to redeem our-selves," my dad solemnly answered my not-so-serious question.

"Come on." I don't know why I was having such a hard time buying their claims, when I'd thought of myself as a vampire for some time. Except that they were my parents, and parents were supposed to be ordinary and respectable. Especially mine, who were boring academics.

But the more I thought about it, the less ridiculous it seemed. My parents were uncommonly beautiful; people always commented on it. They carried themselves with an unusual grace and calmness, excepting their reactions to my most recent behavior, of course. They dedicated them-selves to teaching others how to protect the environment while still feeding the multitudes. They were the only peo-ple whose touch did not give me a single flash. And they were my parents, the ones who'd created me. If I was some kind of supernatural being, why not them? Lately, crazier things had happened.

The thought sobered me up—although I wasn't quite ready to buy the entire notion.

My mom shot my dad a look, and he left the room. My mom and I sat there in an uncomfortable silence as we lis-tened to Dad's slippers clop up and down the attic stairs.

He returned bearing a small wooden box covered in metal designs, kind of like the tin-imprinted, wooden trunks Irish immigrants brought over with them on the ships a couple of centuries ago.

Reaching into her nightgown, my mom pulled out a long gold chain made up of open, circular links. I knew that there was a plain, heavy oval pendant, also gold, on the chain too. As a child, I'd loved to play with it, running it up and down the chain until my mother tired of my game and admonished me to be careful with it. Over the years, I'd grown to see it as my mom's one vanity, her one decoration in a wardrobe of simple, functional clothes. But I was wrong.

She twisted the pendant, and it popped open unexpectedly. The little motion made me jump; I never knew that the pendant was a locket. Then she reached inside, pulled out a small key, and handed it to my dad.

He slid the key into the box's lock and opened it with one deft turn. Moving slowly and carefully, he thumbed through the items inside and removed a yellowed envelope. He placed it in my hands.

The envelope was sealed. Working my finger under the one loose corner, I looked up at my dad for confirmation that I could open it. He nodded. Gingerly, I loosened the flap on the back and peered inside. A stack of what looked like photographs rested within.

I slid them out. They were indeed photographs, all of varying vintages. Some were fairly recent—black and whites from the nineteen forties maybe—and some were so old that they were printed in sepia. Flipping through them quickly at first, I thought they were postcards because they depicted so many exotic locations. They showed the pyramids of Giza in the late eighteen hundreds, the Great Wall of China in the early nineteen hundreds, even the Empire State Building under construction, with an attractive couple in the foreground.

As I examined the pictures more closely, they appeared too amateurish and informal for postcards. The lighting and focus were often blurry, and the centering sometimes seemed a bit off. The more I studied them the more they looked like snapshots of different couples on their holidays. Why were my parents giving me these? Particularly now.

As if reading my thoughts, my dad said softly, "Look closely."

I stared at the pictures, willing them to make some sort of sense. Then I recalled that the couple was identical in every photo. Different hairstyles, different clothes, but otherwise the same couple looking precisely the same for a span of nearly one hundred and fifty years. Only then did I realize that I knew them: they were my parents.

"Oh, so this is supposed to be your proof of immortality, I take it?" I asked. My skepticism had returned.

"You think these are fake?" my mom said. She sounded stunned and a little hurt.

"Anything can be Photoshopped, Mom."

"You think we prepared these so that we could make up an elaborate lie about being angels?" She moved past stunned and on to furious. "And how do you explain your little flying sessions?"

When she put it that way . . . The crazy thing was my parents were the most practical, down-to-earth people I knew. Or thought I knew, anyway. I scrutinized the photographs again. There, among the pictures of all the far-flung destinations was one smallish photo of my parents in period garb staring at each other. The joyous expressions on their faces caught my eye, and I took a closer look. They were seated before the white-washed church on the Tillinghast town green, a familiar enough setting. Except that the church was the only structure in sight; none of the other storefronts and homes that surrounded it had been built yet.

I held up the picture. "This is Tillinghast?"

My dad drew close to the photo, and smiled at the

memory it evoked. "Yes, that is Tillinghast in the late eighteen hundreds." He handed it to my mom. "Remember,
Hannah?"

She smiled back at him. "Yes, we were so happy here,
despite all troubles."

"What troubles?" I asked.

The grin disappeared from her face. "Like many New
England towns in the eighteenth and nineteenth centuries,
Tillinghast suffered from several outbreaks of tuberculosis
and consumption. Some of us who were attempting to find
a path toward redemption visited here in the early days and
tried to bring the many dying over to God. Unfortunately,
these efforts were witnessed by a few Tillinghast towns-
men and mistaken as the work of vampires, as your father
described." The smile resurfaced. "Still, we loved it here.
That's why we came back—when you arrived."

I stared up at my parents, seeing them as if for the very
first time. Suddenly, without warning, I believed them.

"You two are angels. Fallen angels, to be exact." I didn't
intend it to be a question, but a statement. "The good kind."

"Yes," they answered in unison.

"So you can fly and read people's thoughts? By touch or
blood?"

"We could," my mom answered, alone this time.

"What do you mean? I thought you said that angels could do all that stuff."

"They can. But we can no longer do those things. For the most part," my mom said.

"Why not?"

"That part is not really important. We chose a different path."

"What path is that?"

"Part of our path is to teach people ways to care for this earth so it can be saved."

I nodded. "What's the other part of your 'path'?"

"To watch over you," my mom said.

"Me?"

"Yes, you."

What was so special about me that two angels needed to keep an eye on me? Then it dawned on me. Angels weren't supposed to be able to procreate, but my parents obviously 'procreated' me. "Is it because you were able to have a child, even though God—or whoever—banned the angels from conceiving?"

"Something like that, dearest. We have always felt blessed to care for you," my dad said.

"So I'm a fallen angel? Like you two?" Just saying those words aloud, aligning myself with them, made me feel lighter. Less alone. I was shedding the weighty, dark secret I'd been keeping—and living—for the past couple of months.

"Not exactly, Ellie. You are somewhat different from the rest of us, either those that keep to the darkness or those that chose the light."

"But I can do all the things that you described—the flying, the reading of people's thoughts."

"We know. Now."

"What am I?"

My mom stepped in. "We cannot tell you just yet. It isn't time. But we will. Please trust us."

My dad reached over and touched my cheek. "Maybe it's better for you to get some rest, dearest. We can talk more tomorrow and answer some of your questions. At dinner."

Sleep? Who could sleep with all this revelation? The very suggestion made me mad. They wanted me to sleep on a secret they'd kept from me for sixteen years. A major, major secret. I needed answers about my nature, my powers, and my immortality—for God's sake. And I needed them now.

"No way. There is no way you're going to spring all this on me, and then expect me to go to sleep." I was as angry at my parents as I'd ever been.

"We know that you are angry, dearest. It is perfectly understandable under the circumstances. But there's time enough for your questions when you've slept," my dad said. His voice had a curious, singsong quality to it.

I started to object, when all of a sudden, sleep really did seem like the most logical suggestion in the world. My dad took me by the hand and brought me to my bedside. My mom pulled back the quilt and motioned for me to slide into the sheets. I had no choice but to follow them like an obedient child. Even though a tiny voice in my head wondered whether they still had some of those angelic powers of persuasion and were using them on me.

Snuggling down into my covers, I looked up at my parents. My mom cast upon me a smile that could only be described as beatific, like some Madonna. Or maybe I was just seeing angels and saints everywhere.

The last words I remembered hearing before I drifted off into a deep sleep came from my mom. She said, "Ellspeth, try to shroud—in your mind—what you've learned tonight from Michael."

The last thought I remembered thinking before I drifted off into that deep sleep was that it took a curiously long time for them to mention Michael. Especially since he and I were the same.

Twenty-nine

Michael was waiting for me at school the next morning.

"Where were you last night? I was so worried about you," he said before I could even get my locker door open.

I quickly scanned the hall to make sure no one was listening. Fortunately everyone looked just as rushed as I was; I was seriously late for Miss Taunton's class. "My parents caught me," I whispered.

"Caught you?" Inexplicably, he seemed confused.

"Caught me trying to sneak out."

A look of horror crossed his face. "They didn't see you—"

I knew he was about to say "flying," so I cut him off. "No, they didn't see me do that." The words were technically true—if not accurate. My parents knew about my flying; they just didn't witness it last night. Why didn't I tell him?

I wondered why I felt uncertain. I'd woken up confused about what my parents had told me, and mad that they'd kept such secrets from me. But at the same time, I retained that sense of lightness I first experienced when they told me, at the thought I might be part of something better and bigger than myself. That hopeful sensation stayed with me as I got ready for school and drove in with my mom—even when she fended off my relentless questions with assurances that we'd talk later and even when I started to get angry at her withholding explanations. All morning, I could barely contain my excitement to tell Michael what I'd learned about my identity, our identities. Despite my promises to my parents to the contrary.

Yet now that the opportunity was at hand, I wavered. There was something different, even off-putting, in Michael's manner—something I couldn't quite describe— that made me hesitate. And I hadn't hesitated with him for a long time.

"Thank God for that," he said.

"Thank God." I smiled a little; the phrase had taken on new meaning.

He took me by the hand and asked, "Do you think you'd be able to get away after school today? I know it's tough with your grounding and all, but something happened last night. I want to tell you about it."

"I don't know, Michael. The grounding isn't my only problem. After my parents caught me trying to sneak out last night, they specifically told me I couldn't see you anymore."

He withdrew his hand. "Me? Why?"

"They guessed that I was going to meet you. Not that I admitted it."

"Great," he said sarcastically. "Now we'll only be able to see each other during the supervised school hours of eight thirty to three thirty and after midnight. Assuming your parents don't camp out in your bedroom."

"Assuming they don't camp out in my bedroom," I repeated, sadly. Although, given what I knew they knew, I was pretty certain that's just about what they'd be doing.

Michael grabbed my hand again and pulled me away from the throngs of students racing to class. He led me down a dark corridor that led to the empty auditorium. Backing me up into a niche holding a set of double doors, he breathed into my neck. "Ellie, I won't be able to stay away from you at night. One night was hard enough. Say you'll meet me at Ransom Beach after school."

All morning, I'd experienced a sense of lightness, like the black fog in which I'd been living had lifted. But now, with Michael so close, I felt the bloodlust again, along with the intoxication of the darkness. And I knew I'd find a way to meet him after school.

I made it into Miss Taunton's classroom just before the

bell finished ringing. Weaving down the crowded aisle to my seat in the back, I tried to ignore the hateful stares of my classmates. In fact, I tried so hard to ignore them that I tripped on a foot that had been outstretched for that very purpose. I pretended not to hear to delighted giggles— among them, Miss Taunton's—as I picked myself off the floor and dusted off my pants.

Settling into my seat, I rifled through my bag for the paper due on Edith Wharton. The text icon on my cell flashed, a rarity. With my hands still in my bag, I clicked on it. To my surprise, it was from Ruth. *Are u ok?* she asked.

That text was the first time she'd communicated with me since the night of the dance. Immediately, I texted back. *Fine. Used to it. Thx for asking.*

Want to meet for coffee after school? she responded.

I raced to answer her. *Yes!* Just yesterday, if she'd asked me to coffee, I wouldn't have cared. The darkness's hold had been that firm. But now that a sliver of light had poked through the clouds, I felt excitement at reconnecting with Ruth. Plus, I had another reason to be thrilled: I had my way to meet Michael.

I negotiated with my mom for a limited—very limited— exemption from my grounding, a negotiation that required I pass my cell to Ruth for her confirmation that we would be making a quick stop for coffee and that she'd bring me directly home. On the car ride to the Daily Grind, we didn't broach the rift between us. Instead, we talked about our classes and the heaping piles of homework. I waited until we sat side by side in our two favorite club chairs, with steaming coffees in our hands.

"Ruth, I'm really sorry about ruining the dance for you and Jamie."

"It's all right, Ellie. I was furious when it first happened. I mean, I knew that you hadn't actually set up that Facebook page. I knew that Piper and Missy must have done that. But why on earth did you race up to that stage and take credit for such a hateful thing? It seemed so pointless and . . . out of character. And, of course, it totally ruined our night. But I'm not mad about it anymore. I haven't been mad about that for a while."

I didn't want to ask the logical next question, but I had no choice. "What have you been mad about?"

"The way you've changed."

"What do you mean?" Again, the question had to be asked.

"Since the night of the dance, you've become distant and cold. You've been walking around like you're in a different world. I understand that you had to put up some kind of barrier to deal with the anger of the other kids, but with me? Especially when I tried so hard to break through to you."

Now that perplexed me. I knew that I hadn't much cared about anyone but Michael, but I honestly didn't recall any special efforts on Ruth's part to break through my barrier. "I'm sorry, Ruth. I don't know what you're talking about."

"You really don't remember me trying to talk to you after English? Or walking with you to the school assembly?" She sounded baffled.

I shook my head; I had no recollection of such things. Then, for the first time since all the madness, I touched her hand. In a rush, I watched the past few weeks through Ruth's eyes. I witnessed my rejection of her overtures, felt the sadness and loneliness that overcame her with each rebuffed approach, and experienced her nightly tears. I could tell that there was more, but Ruth quickly withdrew her hand.

I started sobbing. "Ruth, I am so sorry. I—"

She interrupted with a hug. "Ellie, I know you're going through something difficult, something obviously I can't understand. Let's talk about it when you've calmed down, okay?"

Squeezing me tighter, she said excitedly, "Can I tell you all about me and Jamie instead?"

We spent the next half hour chatting like nothing bad

had transpired between us. I heard all about her budding romance, and I loved watching the happiness in her face. It made me wish that I was normal, that Michael and I could hang out with my best friend and her new boyfriend like ordinary teenagers.

Ruth glanced at her watch and jumped up. She'd made plans to meet Jamie at the library, but would drive me home first.

"Ruth, I have a favor to ask, but I'm hesitant after everything I've put you through."

"Ellie, you are still my closest friend. I'll always be happy to help you. You know that."

"It will require that you disobey my mom's specific request to bring me home after coffee."

"All right," she said hesitantly.

"Would you mind dropping me at Ransom Beach when we leave? And not telling my parents if it ever comes up?"

THIRTY

Ransom Beach looked more isolated and less welcoming than I remembered. The craggy cliffs seemed to drop more precipitously into the white-capped ocean, and there was not a soul in sight, it being late fall. From the inside of the car, Ruth and I could tell that the beach was colder and windier than town. We could even hear the loud cry of the seagulls through the closed car windows, and they sounded lonely, rather than the normal friendly harbinger of summer. The whole scenario made Ruth visibly uncomfortable.

"What are you guys doing out here?" she asked skeptically.

"We just like to walk along the beach," I lied. I felt a little bad about it, but being with Michael was more important than not telling a white lie.

"In this weather?" Ruth wasn't buying it.

Before answering, I hung my head down. I didn't think I could tell her yet another lie while looking her in the face.

"It's the one place we can really be alone to talk."

I could tell Ruth didn't believe me, but she wasn't going to challenge me any further. Still, she refused to let me out of the car until Michael appeared. We spent several long minutes making small talk while she looked at the car clock—she didn't want to keep Jamie waiting, I could tell— and I scanned the otherwise empty road for Michael's car. When he finally arrived, we both let out a sigh of relief.

She was reluctant to go. "Are you sure you'll be all right, Ellie?"

I smiled assuredly. "Of course, Ruth."

"It doesn't seem particularly safe out here . . . ," she said.

"I'll be with Michael."

"Okay. But don't be afraid to call if you need me." She paused, then added with a smile, "And please go home within the hour like we promised your mom. I don't want her mad at me. She can be scary."

I gave her a hug—thankful for the ride and the bridge back toward friendship—and hopped out of the car. Immediately, I was grateful she hadn't let me out sooner. The salty air was bracing and strong, practically slapping me in the face with its cold dampness. If I wasn't so confident in my flying skills, I might have clung to the road instead of braving the cliffside path nearest to Michael's car.

Ruth was still waiting, so I raced over to his car. Waving

good-bye, I opened the door and slid in. Straightaway, Michael pulled me toward him, and over the gearshift, he kissed me. I'd been feeling guilty about deceiving my parents and using Ruth to help me, but his lips and his hands wiped all that guilt away. I needed to be with him.

"So where are we going? In an hour, I have to be home."

"Actually, I thought we might stay here, down in the cove." He smiled. "It's where we had one of our first dates, after all."

I laughed. "You're calling that a date now?"

He laughed too. "So are you game? Or is it too cold for you?"

I could tell he was daring me. After all these weeks where I taunted him and pushed him, he was turning the tables back on me. I had to rise to the occasion. "It depends on how we're getting down there," I answered coquettishly.

"I think it might be the right conditions for an afternoon flight."

We'd never flown in daylight before. It was too risky. But if ever a safe time and place existed for the gamble, Ransom Beach in late fall was it. "Let's go," I said.

Checking to make sure Ruth was gone, we got out of the car and walked over to the edge of the cliff. For a moment, that first, terrifying experience of watching Michael jump from the very spot—not knowing that he could fly—revisited me. I felt a little dizzy at the intensity of the memory, and I stopped to steady myself.

"You haven't become afraid of heights overnight, have you?" Michael asked, teasing me again.

I squared my shoulders and looked down the sixty-foot drop. "Of course not." Just to prove my point, I grabbed his hand and dove.

Flying during the day was different. All the shapes and sounds and smells we normally guessed at were clearly discernible. All the hidden dangers were made apparent. Daylight made the experience more exciting and more frightening—simultaneously. By the time we landed on the sand, I wanted more.

But Michael declined my invitation for another flight. He wanted to stay in the cove. Its protective boulders made the temperature surprisingly warm, and Michael's arms made it even warmer. So instead, we stood for a long minute in our sheltered spot, holding each other and staring out at the rough sea.

"There's something I want to tell you—need to tell you—about last night," he whispered softly in my ear.

He had mentioned this earlier. But, in the chaos of the day, I hadn't given it much thought. Particularly since I had my own news that I'd decided to share with him.

"There's something I need to tell you, too," I said.

"I think I should go first," he persisted.

"All right." I suddenly felt uneasy and sick, like he was about to confess that he'd hooked up with another girl last night.

Michael took a deep breath and opened his lips to speak, when—over Michael's shoulders—I saw another person amble down the beach in our direction. A man. He wore jeans and a fleece, but he was barefoot and had his shoes slung casually over his shoulder as if going for a beach stroll on a beautiful summer day. What was he doing out here?

I placed my finger on Michael's lips and said, "Wait. Someone's coming."

He craned his neck to see who it was. Spinning back to face me, he clutched me tighter—as if he was worried I'd fly away—and said, "It's okay, Ellie. He's here to meet us. He is what I wanted to tell you about."

Even though Michael's words registered in my head and he intended them to be a comfort, I couldn't stop staring warily at the man as he came closer and his face became more distinct. The blond hair, the blue eyes, the handsome, chiseled features—I knew I'd seen him before.

He was the guy in the coffee shop several weeks ago, the one I'd bumped into. The one that Ruth couldn't take her eyes off of. The guy who stood by Missy's side at the Fall Dance, and the one I saw in shadows in flashes. He was Zeke.

What on earth was he doing out here? Meeting us?

The guy noticed my gaze, and smiled that creepy, disconcerting smile. And I got really, really scared.

The urge to escape became irrepressible. I felt my shoulder blades start to lift and expand, just like they did before flying, though now the motion was involuntary. Michael must have sensed it, because his grip tightened. Trying to wrench out of his grasp, I dug my nails into his arms. "Michael, what's going on?"

"Ellie, his name is Ezekiel. And he's going to tell us who we are."

THIRTY-ONE

"Who are you?" I asked this "Ezekiel," as I tried to shake off Michael. Why was Michael holding me in a vise grip so I could listen to this guy?

"Ellspeth, allow me to introduce myself. My name is Ezekiel. It is a pleasure to finally meet you, although I apologize for the circumstances." Zeke—or Ezekiel—said, as if we were being introduced over high tea at Bar Harbor's finest hotel rather than on a deserted beach on a freezing cold evening while my boyfriend held me down. All the while, he kept that strange smile pasted on his face.

"Where's your friend, Missy?" I asked, as I struggled to free myself from Michael.

"I am sorry for my unfortunate association with your classmate Missy. I entered into that relationship with the hopes it might provide me with an easy introduction to you and Michael. Sadly, that was not to be the case. But I stayed with her because I saw she could serve other purposes." His language had a formal, almost antiquated, feel to it.

Suddenly I understood why Missy had been so friendly to me at the beginning of school. It was an effort by this Ezekiel to get to us through her. And I thought I knew what he meant by the "other purposes" that Missy served.

"Did you put Missy up to the Facebook stunt?" I asked, having seen him in those flashes. Not that he'd know about them, of course.

"You showed yourself to be quite the savior in that incident, Ellspeth. And you showed me quite a lot about yourself in the process."

"You didn't answer my question. Did you orchestrate that whole sickening thing?"

He sighed, as if disappointed by the inquiry. "No, Ellspeth. I did not force Missy to perpetrate the Facebook stunt, as you have called it. Missy did not act outside her own nature and she did not act at my behest. I will admit to fostering her nature and her Facebook plan as the incident afforded me an important insight. . . . It allowed me to see how you would behave when faced with a truly soulless act. And I saw that, while you were willing to sacrifice yourself to protect the potential victims of Missy's game, you were not immune to the lure of the darkness that emanated from it." Ezekiel smiled, evidently pleased by his remote handiwork and my reaction to his test. "But you should know that I was no puppeteer of Missy, Ellspeth. You must have seen that she acted of her own accord—in your visions."

Like ice, my blood froze in my veins. "How did you know about those?"

"I know what you are and what you can do. Therefore, I assume you saw how her plan unfolded, Ellspeth."

Michael finally spoke. "Ellie, listen to what Ezekiel just said. He knows what we are and what we can do. He can help us understand who we are." Was this the reason that Michael was acting so deferentially toward this Ezekiel? Even if Michael believed that Ezekiel had the answers, it was no excuse for his iron grip, for his betrayal of me.

Ezekiel interjected, his tone still becalming. "It is quite all right, Michael. I think you best release Ellspeth from your embrace."

As if obeying a command, Michael's arms slackened. I faced Ezekiel alone, thoroughly exposed to his fearsomeness.

Ezekiel spoke to Michael, but stared directly at me. "Ellspeth's reaction is perfectly understandable. She does not know who I am. She does not even know who she is. Yet. But I am very much looking forward to sharing with her the uniqueness of her—"

"I don't need you to tell me who I am." It was my turn to

interject. Thanks to my parents, I had some understanding of my identity. Some.

"Ellie, please," Michael begged me—to listen and defer. I felt like I didn't even know Michael. He seemed almost drugged by the very presence of this Ezekiel.

I spun around toward him. Drugged or not, how dare he? "Why should I? You've dragged me to Ransom Beach under false pretenses—once again. I have no reason to trust you, or him." I was so thankful that I hadn't shared my parents' secrets with him.

Michael started to stammer out another objection, but Ezekiel interrupted. "Michael, of course Ellspeth is mistrustful. Once she learns everything that you have learned, she will undoubtedly relinquish her suspicions. She will come to understand—as you have—that I am only here to help you both."

Even though my instincts told me to flee, I knew I would stay. I wanted to hear Ezekiel's explanation of my "uniqueness," to compare it with the story my parents had told me. So I stood firm in the face of his devouring gaze, and waited. I would listen to what he had to say but I would not react. I would take the knowledge I'd garnered from him and return to my parents—with my new information in hand. And they would help me make sense of everything; they would tell me all the details they'd withheld last night. That was my plan, anyway.

Ezekiel acknowledged my momentary acquiescence with a self-satisfied smile. It was the smile of one used to getting what he asked for.

He began. "Last night, I came upon Michael. Alone. He was scared and full of queries, so I answered them. Much as a parent answers the pleas of his child. Because, in many ways, Michael is my child. As are you, Ellspeth.

"You and Michael are born from the same source as me. You fly. You can read and influence the thoughts of others, through touch and blood. You know you are different from the others. Better. But what are you?

"Michael tells me that you have resisted the label of vampire, though all the characteristics seem to fit. How right you were to resist this moniker. The name 'vampire' is given by humans to beings such as ourselves—out of ignorance. You can see, of course, from whence the vampire legend sprung. The flying, the blood, the sheer incomprehensibility of our powers, would give rise to the fairy tale of the vampire.

"But you and Michael are not vampires. Nor am I. Ellspeth, we are select beings, born to lead mankind. And I will show you and Michael the way."

Ezekiel paused dramatically. I guessed that he wanted me to swoon or gush excitedly over his speech. Maybe those were the reactions he usually received. But, in truth, it sounded like the story my parents had told me the night before. Minus the bit about leading mankind. Yet that bit was beginning to give me a good sense of who Ezekiel was. He was sounding more and more like an unrepentant fallen angel, and I was getting more and more frightened.

As Ezekiel waited for my response, he stared into my eyes. "Your parents have told you a different tale about your origin," he finally said. It wasn't a question; it was a statement.

"How did you know?" I asked.

"It is certainly not as if they told me. It has been years since I've had contact with your parents, and they have no idea that I've been in Tillinghast. I know that they've told you a different tale about your origins because I have had centuries—no, millennia—of experience reading faces. I can see that you are not surprised by what I am sharing with you. Your parents are the only ones who could have told you part of this tale."

"Her parents?" Michael asked, as if jolting awake from his trance.

Ezekiel turned to him. "Ellspeth hasn't told you?"

"No," Michael said slowly.

"I had planned on telling you, Michael. Before you sprung all this on me," I said defensively. I didn't know why

I felt the need to justify myself to him, after the stunt he pulled.

"Be wary of what Hananel and Daniel tell you, Ellspeth," Ezekiel said. "After all, they are not your real parents."

Hananel. That was what Michael's mother had called my mom. "Of course they're my real parents."

"To be sure, they have raised you since your birth. From the looks of you, my dear, they have performed that role wonderfully. But Hananel and Daniel played no hand in conceiving you, carrying you, or birthing you."

"You're lying."

He sighed, as if it pained him to bring me such distressing news. "I wish I were lying, my dear Ellspeth. But you see, I was there on the day of your birth. And neither Hananel nor Daniel are your parents."

I needed to know for certain if he was telling the truth. Even though I shivered at the thought of getting close to Ezekiel, I needed to touch him. I needed to see inside his mind.

I wondered if he would allow it. Then I remembered my dad's description of the fallen angels' powers of persuasion and realized that Ezekiel was probably trying to gain control over my mind. Just as he'd seemingly done to Michael. Ezekiel was continuing to use that sing-song voice, certain that he was influencing me.

I saw my opportunity. Acting as if he swayed me, I approached him.

"There have always been inconsistencies in their stories of my birth, discrepancies that never made sense," I said.

"I am not surprised."

"They are not my parents? Really?" As if convinced by his words, I allowed my eyes to well up with very real tears. Tears I'd been holding back from Michael's betrayal.

"Really, dear."

"So I can't trust what they've told me about myself?"

"No, Ellspeth. I am sorry to tell you that you cannot trust the representations of Hananel and Daniel."

"But you will become a parent to us? Michael and I will not be alone? You will show us the way?"

He smiled; this was the reaction he sought. "I will indeed, Ellspeth."

I smiled back at him and drew even closer to his blond hair and blue eyes and his unusual, incense-like scent. "I'm so pleased," I whispered.

"As am I, my dear," he whispered back. Then I touched him.

Thirty-two

The hatred I witnessed in the hearts and minds of my classmates after the Facebook incident was kindergarten stuff in comparison to the darkness of Ezekiel's spirit. Even the malice I'd seen in Missy could not compare. Through his eyes, I watched scene after scene of dominance and degradation, where he'd concocted ingenious and sickening ways to ensnare the attention—and then the souls—of mankind. He was relentless in reaching his nefarious tentacles into human beings' lives—births, marriages, illnesses, deaths, educations, businesses, governments, technology, warfare, money, you name it. Ezekiel would not rest until mankind's thoughts and desires were his own.

He delighted at each conquest, no matter how small or large. For each victory turned another soul away from any hint of goodness. Ezekiel was a fallen angel, and if you bought into the biblical tale, he was punishing God for casting him out. And he would never, ever stop.

His was the darkness that had crept into my soul and mind after the Fall Dance. I wondered if it had crept in through my tasting of Missy's blood. Had she sampled Ezekiel's, and did she carry his blood in her veins?

I did not think I could tolerate the malevolence of Ezekiel's thoughts or, worse, his deeds anymore. He'd performed and arranged countless acts of betrayal, deception, seduction, even murder—some with his own hands, some using the hands of others. I couldn't survive the onslaught a second longer. Then suddenly it stopped. Ezekiel realized what I was doing and shut down his mind.

I opened my eyes and looked directly into his. In that moment, he understood that I saw him—as no one had every truly seen him before. Why couldn't Michael see Ezekiel's evil? Had Ezekiel corrupted him before he had a chance? If Ezekiel had frightened me before, he now terrified me.

But the flash had given me a moment of clarity and freedom, and I flew.

I had never flown as fast or as high. Propelling upward, I sped past the boulders that comprised the sheltering cove, the sharp rock face into which the path was cut, and spiky precipice that made up the cliff top. I desperately needed to make it to the level rock overlooking Ransom Beach before Ezekiel or Michael. Otherwise, the vantage point of the Ransom Beach cliff top would provide them with the precise direction of my route. Once I figured it out.

I touched down on the top of the cliff. For a moment, I saw nothing but gray skies and grayer rocks and the black asphalt of the highway. No silvery-white of Michael's or Ezekiel's hair. I exhaled in relief.

Too soon. I felt the earth shudder beneath my feet, and suddenly Ezekiel was there.

"Ellspeth," he said with his awful smile; it was like seeing the skeleton under his skin. "Where do you think you are going, dear?"

When Ezekiel walked toward me, I realized that he wasn't alone. Michael stood to his right.

They were converging on me. Slowly but deliberately. As I backed away, I realized just how much they looked alike. It clouded my thinking for a minute, but then I refocused. My choices were limited: move backward to the cliff edge from which I'd just alighted, or head out onto the deserted highway. I opted for the road and the slim chance that a car would appear. Not that a vehicle and driver could stop this duo.

"Ellspeth, there's nowhere else to go. Nowhere else will you be understood and appreciated for who you are," Ezekiel said.

"We are your true family," Michael echoed Ezekiel. What was happening to him?

"You belong with us, Ellspeth. You were born to rule, with Michael and me at your side." Ezekiel kept using that lulling tone, despite my read of him. I bet it lured a lot of people to him, but just now it wasn't working. Not that I'd point that out. I'd hate to see what tactic he'd try instead.

"Please, Ellie. You know that you and I were meant to be together," Michael piped in. How could he have joined up with this monster? Did he not see what I saw?

I kept retreating as they continued their slow advance toward me. I didn't know how to fend them off or where to go. Unfortunately, comforting thoughts of home kept penetrating my consciousness before I could lock them out. I longed to be with my parents, and Ezekiel must have read the yearning on my face.

"Do you think of returning to Hananel and Daniel, Ellspeth? They can no longer protect you. And your presence will only bring them harm."

"What do you mean?" I stopped.

"Didn't they tell you their little secret while they were divulging yours?"

I shook my head, sick at the thought of what he was about to say.

"No? Hananel and Daniel surrendered their immortality when they agreed to raise you as their child."

THIRTY-THREE

"Ruth, you said I could call if I needed you. I really, really need you."

To her credit, Ruth didn't ask what happened or why I needed help. She just asked where I was, and said she'd pick me up in twenty minutes.

Twenty minutes? Twenty minutes sounded like an eternity when I knew how fast Ezekiel and Michael could travel if they wanted. I prayed that Ezekiel meant what he said just before I took off: "Let her go, Michael. She will return to us when she is ready."

Rainwater pooled at my feet as I slid my cell back into my bag. I wiped off my face and hair as best I could with a dry T-shirt from my bag, and looked around the kitschy general store, The Maine Event. In summertime, when the tourists flocked to the beaches and even the locals became regulars at the seaside hangouts, this place swarmed with visitors. Now, manned by a single attendant, it didn't exactly have the comfort of crowds. But I didn't spot a lot of other options as I skirted this isolated stretch of highway, especially once it started to storm.

Trying to look occupied, I strolled around the store. I spun carousels of postcards and examined shelves with seashells and local preserves. The attendant gave me a curious once-over, so I hoped that I looked more appropriate—and interested—than I felt. My mind whirred with the horrors I'd seen through Ezekiel's eyes and the narrowness of my escape.

After exactly twenty minutes, I heard the bell over the front door ring. My stomach lurched. I wasn't sure whether it was my savior Ruth or my persecutors.

Thank God it was Ruth.

She raced over. "Are you okay? You look terrible."

"I'm fine. Really I am."

"Did Michael do something to you?"

I knew that would be her presumption; after all, she'd looked reluctant to drop me off with Michael at Ransom Beach less than two hours ago. In formulating my reason for the emergency pickup, I had decided to play on that assumption. "We just had a fight. And I didn't trust him to bring me home straightaway."

"I understand." She gave me a hug and pulled me toward the door. "Come on, I'll take you home."

Home. I wished I could go home, but I couldn't. I would have to enlist Ruth's unwitting aid once more—to protect myself and my parents. And her, for that matter.

We drove in silence until I asked her about Jamie. Her face lit up as she described how smart he was and how helpful with her homework. I kept her talking until we neared the Tillinghast town green. When we pulled alongside the whitewashed town church, I asked her to stop the car for a minute.

"Ruth, I'm going to ask for an enormous favor. The biggest favor I've ever asked of you. And I'm not going to be able to tell you why."

"Okay," she said hesitantly.

"Can you please take me to the train station? And not tell my parents or Michael. Or anyone else who might ask."

She paused, weighing very carefully whether or not to utter her next words. "Ellie, I know."

"Know what?"

"I know about you and Michael—and the flying."

I was stunned into speechlessness.

Ruth looked down at her hands, almost embarrassed by what she'd said and how she knew. "I told you earlier that I just didn't understand the whole Facebook thing. It seemed totally out of character for you, and you acted so different afterward. So I started eavesdropping here and there. I overheard you saying to Michael that you'd see him later that night—even though you were grounded. It got me wondering whether you two were sneaking out, and whether Michael was the reason you changed so much. So I began to follow you—at night. That's when I saw you fly for the first time."

"You saw us." I couldn't believe my ears.

"Yes." She smiled despite herself. "It was really amazing to watch."

I shook my head in disbelief.

"Ellie, does the trip to the train station have something to do with your flying?"

"Yes, in a way."

She paused again. It was strange for me to watch my best friend of seven years acting so uncomfortable around me. "What are you, Ellie?"

I didn't have an answer, although I wished desperately that I did. "Would you believe me if I told you that I honestly don't know?"

Reaching out toward me, she clasped my hand. "After seeing you two fly, I'd believe anything."

I didn't want to push her along, but I knew I was running out of time. "So you'll take me to the train station?"

"Do you really need to go? I don't know what I'll do without you, Ellie. Especially now that you are back. The real you, I mean."

Tears started welling up in my eyes at the idea of leaving my poor parents behind. And Ruth. And Tillinghast. But I knew I couldn't stay. Ezekiel had warned me.

"I have to go. It's in everyone's best interest," I said, knowing that Ruth couldn't possibly comprehend—or believe—the danger I'd be thrusting upon Tillinghast if I didn't leave.

"Take me with you, Ellie," she said suddenly. Although I could tell she'd been mustering up the courage to make her request.

"You don't want to be a part of this. I promise you."

"Ellie, I don't know what you are, but I know you are more than human." She started to cry too. "I've seen up close what it means to be human. With my mom's death. And I don't want to end up like that. I'd rather be like you."

Watching Ruth cry made me cry harder. "Oh, Ruth, even if I wanted to, I couldn't turn you into whatever I am. And anyway, I don't think my differences make me immune from dying."

We hugged each other for a long time. Ruth broke away first, and turned the car back on. "I guess I should take you to the train station."

THIRTY-FOUR

I walked into the back entrance of the sleepy Tillinghast train station feeling more alone than ever before. It wasn't because the station was empty except for a lone ticket agent or because I was uncertain about my destination. It was because I was truly on my own.

I didn't know when—or how—my solitude would end. I couldn't see or even contact my parents until I could be certain I wouldn't cause them harm. The same applied to Ruth. As for Michael, well, he had chosen Ezekiel over me; he was gone. And there was no one else.

As I stared up at the train destination board, a tear ran down my cheek. For a split second, I was glad to be alone. I didn't want anyone to see my weakness. I needed to be strong to face the coming days.

Wiping the tear away, I concentrated on the board. I scanned the list of trains slated to leave the station in the morning, but immediately rejected those as departing too late. I couldn't chance staying overnight in the station. I didn't doubt that Ezekiel could descend upon me if he so chose, but I did not want my parents to find me and suffer Ezekiel's wrath.

Then I noticed that one last train was due into the station that night, just after eight P.M. Called the Downeaster, the train stopped at the Tillinghast station in fifteen minutes. It would arrive in Boston in about three hours—Boston. I had my destination; it couldn't have been more perfect if I'd planned it.

I waited until the station agent stepped away from his post to buy my ticket from the ticket machine with cash. Purchasing it from the automated teller rather than the agent seemed wiser. I'd gain some lead time if Ezekiel and Michael changed their collective minds and followed me, instead of waiting as Ezekiel initially instructed.

Ticket in hand, I headed into the ladies' room to wait until I heard the train pull into the station. I didn't want to give the agent any additional time to identify me. I paced around restlessly, listening intently for the train and making a few critical internet searches before I tossed my cell phone. I didn't want anyone to trace me that way either.

As I jotted down the vital pieces of information from my research, I heard the chug of the train. Then I threw my cell into the trash.

Peering out the bathroom door, I didn't see the agent anywhere. I darted from the bathroom into the train, quickly grabbed a seat, and buried myself in a book I snatched from my bag. I didn't want to look as if I'd just boarded, in case the Tillinghast agent peeked in.

I didn't really exhale until the train pulled away from the Tillinghast station. Only then, and only surreptitiously, did I assess my fellow travelers. In the rear of the car sat two businessmen talking about a meeting they had the next morning with a prospective client. In the occupied seats closest to mine were a few kids that looked like they were headed back to college. I kept an eye on them. Their sweatshirts, backpacks, and other paraphernalia bore the Harvard logo, and I thought they might prove useful.

The door separating the cars suddenly slid open, and I jumped. It was only the conductor ready to take my ticket. As I pretended to rifle through my bag so I wouldn't have to look directly at him, I handed it over. He punched it and then placed the stub in the slot above my head. His business completed, he left the car.

I had three hours until we reached Boston. Three hours to prepare. Three hours to map out a game plan.

I decided to start by assessing my resources—whatever was in my bag. I hadn't exactly planned my departure in advance, so I was limited to what I carried. When we traveled, my parents always insisted that I carry on my person all the necessities should I ever be separated from them—a couple hundred dollars, identification, a toiletry bag with essentials, credit cards, and an ATM card that now I'd have to avoid using except when absolutely necessary. I'd gotten into the habit of carrying these things. Lucky that I did. It made me prepared for a day like this. Maybe that was their intention all along; maybe they knew a day like this would come.

Thinking about my parents—and I would always consider them my mom and dad, birth parents or not—made my eyes start to well up again. I wasn't mad at them anymore for keeping secrets; I understood that they were just trying to protect me. They'd even given up their immortality to shield me. And even though Ezekiel couldn't be trusted, I believed what he said about their sacrificed immortality when I thought how my parents had aged in the past sixteen years after staying youthful for over a hundred years of pictures.

But if they weren't my real parents, who were? Were my real parents still alive? Why did Hananel and Daniel have to raise me? Who did they make that arrangement with?

They would be worried sick about me by now. I wondered if they would file a police report or conduct a search for me on their own. I hoped they still had some residual powers on which they could draw.

But I didn't have the luxury of emotions, and I certainly didn't want to draw attention to myself by crying. So I took a pad of paper and pen from my bag and scribbled down all my questions.

The train rocked back and forth and stopped from time to time during the three hours to Boston. But I was so engrossed, these events hardly registered with me. By the time the train screeched into Boston's North Station, I had made a list of the questions I had about my nature and future.

I looked down at my notes:

1. What was I? My gifts sounded a lot like the ones Dad had described for angels. Did that mean I was an angel, fallen or good? Or was I some other kind of supernatural being? Mom had said I was "somewhat different" from the angels.

2. What was my purpose? Dad said that the angels were meant to use their gifts—flying, flashes, and persuasive powers—to guide souls to God. Was that what I was supposed to be doing with mine? After all, before the whole Facebook thing, I'd experienced that intense compulsion to help others. But Mom and Dad had hinted that I had some kind of special role. What was that role?

3. Who was Ezekiel, and why was he so interested in

me? I had guessed that he was one of the fallen angels, but not the kind seeking redemption. If so, why didn't he just use his persuasive powers to force me to his side? It seemed like he had some kind of influence over Michael in that way. And how did Ezekiel find me and Michael anyway?

4. If I could even believe Ezekiel about my parents, who were my birth parents? And where were they? And why had Hannah (I couldn't think of her as Hananel) and Daniel agreed to raise me?

5. Had I lost Michael to Ezekiel forever?

I prayed that these questions might be answered in Boston, because, without the answers, I was paralyzed. And terribly confused. But armed with this information, I might stand a chance against Ezekiel, and might be able to protect my parents in the process.

The students riding along with me were headed to the same place, so I followed in their wake. I hoped that it would make me seem like just another college student. I trailed along after them as they connected into Boston's subway system, the T, and hopped on a Red Line train headed for Cambridge. Nowhere along the way did I sense that I was being tracked.

I alighted when the students did and tagged along—at a distance—as they walked to their campus. As they filed into their dorms, I started to get concerned. What was I going to do until tomorrow morning? I wasn't worried about staying awake until sunrise—I'd had too many long nights with Michael to worry about that—but staying safe and inconspicuous.

Then I remembered we had passed an all-night coffee shop when we walked from the T stop toward the dorms. It seemed to cater to students with its late hours and free internet. So I headed back in that direction.

When I opened the door, I saw that it was populated by bleary-eyed undergrads studying and cranking out papers, fueled by coffee and cookies. I knew I had my waiting spot.

I had nearly nine hours to kill until nine A.M.—when I could try to meet with Professor McMaster.

Thirty-five

I didn't know why I felt so certain that a man I'd merely read about on the internet could answer my questions. Especially since his specialty was vampires, and I'd come to believe that I was something else entirely. But I was desperate for answers, and desperation bred overconfidence, I guessed. I thought that if he could just tell me what I was—and my purpose—I'd be able to make sense of this madness.

When morning came, I cleaned up as best I could in the coffee shop bathroom and left my little haven for a bookstore, camping out at a Dunkin' Donuts afterward. It offered an excellent view of the entrance to the building where Professor McMaster held office hours. At exactly two minutes to nine, I watched as a disheveled-looking elderly man with frizzy gray hair raced into the building. At first, the man caught my attention because he was seriously underdressed for the cold, wearing only a tatty-looking blazer tossed on over a button-down shirt. Then I realized that the man resembled the photo from the Harvard website, even though he looked significantly older. I decided that it was definitely Professor McMaster.

I waited two minutes, and then followed him into the building. I didn't want to bombard him, but I needed to be the first in line for his nine A.M. to eleven A.M. office hours. Instead of taking the elevator, as he did, I climbed the two flights of stairs to his office. Passing by what looked like a departmental secretary, I walked directly to his door— which was closed.

Double-checking the posted office hours to be sure I had the right time, I knocked on the door. Other than a rustle of papers and the squeak of a desk chair, I didn't hear anything. So I knocked again.

"I heard you the first time. I'll be with you in a moment," a gravelly, very slightly accented voice answered. And he didn't sound happy.

"Thanks," I said sheepishly. This wasn't exactly the start for which I'd hoped.

A few minutes later, I heard a series of locks jangle. Then the door creaked open, just a sliver. "Come in, come in," he said impatiently.

I slid through the small opening Professor McMaster provided. He then closed and locked the door behind us.

After the greeting I'd received and the frazzled state of the professor, I wasn't exactly excited to be in a locked office with him. But what were my choices?

I didn't want to be presumptuous and take the seat opposite his desk, so I stood there until invited. He made some grumbling noises as he stepped over the piles of papers littering the floor to get to his desk chair. Once he settled in, he just stared at me with his surprisingly bright and clear brown eyes.

"What are you waiting for?" He gestured to the guest chair.

I hustled over to the battered wooden chair and sat down. I had planned on introducing myself as a Harvard student writing for the daily newspaper—*The Harvard Crimson*—that wanted to conduct an interview of him. I'd even bought and put on a Harvard sweatshirt, and carried a copy of the *Crimson* on top of my notebook. But the professor's manner was so gruff and odd, I hesitated. Much to the professor's irritation.

He stuck out his open hand in my direction. "Come on, miss. Have you got it or not?"

"Got what?"

"Your seminar paper. Today's office hours are reserved exclusively for my Eastern European Myths and Legends seminar students."

He saw my blank stare and squinted at me. "You are in my seminar, are you not?"

"No, I'm not. I am actually a—"

He cut me off. "Then I must ask you to leave. You may come back during my regular office hours on Friday."

"I'm afraid I really can't wait until Friday, Professor McMaster."

"I'm afraid you do not have a choice, Miss—"

"Faneuil."

"Come along, Miss Faneuil. There are no imminent deadlines in my other two courses, so you will have to wait until Friday. The seminar students have priority."

I launched into my little plan. I thought I'd play on his vanity with *The Harvard Crimson* interview—everybody liked to talk about themselves—and then sneak in my questions. That way, I wouldn't scare him off. I just kept my fingers crossed that he wouldn't ask for any *Crimson* identification.

"I promise I won't take up too much of your time, Professor McMaster. I'm a writer with *The Harvard Crimson*, and we would like to do an interview of you for our magazine section. I would've set up an appointment with your secretary, but we have an unexpected opening today and we would love to fill it with an interview of you." I looked down at my notepad as if consulting some notes. "My staff told me that we've never done a formal interview of you, and we'd like to rectify that situation."

The professor's face softened. I could tell that he really didn't want to do an interview, but felt obliged. He said, "My apologies, Miss Faneuil."

"I'm the one who should apologize, Professor McMaster. As I said, I really should have made an appointment with your secretary. Especially since this seems like a really busy time."

"It is indeed. I am fully committed to student appointments through the afternoon. However, I can offer you fifteen minutes right now, before the first student starts clamoring for his meeting."

"I really appreciate it, Professor." I looked back down at my notepad of "interview" questions, and said, "Let's not waste a minute."

Quickly, I asked him a series of basic questions about his background and areas of expertise. He was responsive enough, although he was visibly uncomfortable. His discomfort increased when I started on the questions I really wanted to know about—the characteristics of vampires. And what—if anything—he knew about other supernatural creatures.

He interrupted me. "Miss Faneuil, I informed you that

I could spare fifteen minutes. I believe that I kept to my promise. I cannot offer you a moment more."

The professor stood up abruptly and came around to my side of the desk, presumably to escort me back to the locked door. As he took me by the hand to lead me out of his office, I got a flash from his touch. It was mild, but astonishing in the breadth and potency of its information. And not surprising in its contents given that we'd just been talking about his upbringing. I didn't want to use what I'd learned to get his attention—that seemed too fallen, for my purposes. But I had no choice.

"I'm afraid that I'm going to have to insist on a few more minutes . . . Professor Laszlof."

THIRTY-SIX

The professor recoiled from my touch, as if I'd burned him. "What did you call me?"

"Istvan Laszlof. That was your given name, wasn't it?"

He didn't speak. Maybe he couldn't. It had probably been fifty years since anyone had called him by his birth name.

When I touched him, I learned that he had been born in Eastern Europe in the nineteen thirties, as Istvan Laszlof. He came to this country with excellent credentials as a historian and spoke near-perfect English—but no one would admit him into their doctoral program at that time. They'd rather see a former adherent of Communism mopping the floors of their hallowed halls. Not one to be cowed and so thirsty for knowledge that nothing could stop him, Istvan bought himself a new identity and reapplied to all the top programs as Raymond McMaster. If the truth about his falsification became known, Professor McMaster's career would be destroyed.

"Who told you that?"

"It doesn't matter."

"It most certainly does." His naturally unpleasant tone was getting nasty.

"Professor, I have no intention of sharing your secret with anyone else. I just want a few more minutes of your time."

"Miss Faneuil, if you do not tell me where you learned this information, I will not give you the time you want."

Now I was getting mad. I just wanted to talk to him— why did it require telling him all my secrets? But what were my options? "You just told me about Istvan Laszlof."

"I don't understand."

I spoke slowly, wanting to soften my next statement as much as possible. "I learned about your origins as Istvan Laszlof by touching you just now. Professor McMaster, I'm not like other people. I can see and do things that would probably shock you. I didn't tell you about Istvan Laszlof to scare you—as I have no intention of telling anyone else— but because it seemed the only way to get a little more of your time."

Trembling, he walked back behind his desk and sat down. "That's really all you want? Just to talk?" He looked very skeptical.

"Yes, that's really all I want. I'm not here not to frighten you; I'm here for your help."

In an effort to reassemble the shattered pieces of Professor McMaster and store away Istvan Laszlof, he smoothed his wild hair and straightened his shirt before speaking. After taking a deep, steadying breath, he gestured that I should take a seat and said, "I'd be happy to assist you, then, Miss Faneuil. Though, I must confess, I do not know very much about psychics. Vampires are my area of expertise."

"Oh, Professor McMaster, I'm not a psychic."

"What are you, Miss Faneuil?"

"I am hoping you can tell me what I am."

He appeared relieved at my request. "I am little used to classifying people."

I wasn't about to relinquish my hope so readily. "Yes, but you have some familiarity with creatures that aren't human?"

"I do," he admitted reluctantly.

"And you believe in the existence of such beings? Including vampires?"

"Yes. I have had the acquaintance of a few beings that I would consider to be actual vampires. Hence, the necessity for the locks on my office door; one can enter and exit my office only by my own hand. Evil must be kept at bay as best it can."

"I understand," I said, although I knew that no lock could keep someone like Ezekiel "at bay."

He quickly added, "But, in most cases, the individuals who have made such claims are only humans whose perceived differences can be explained by a thorough understanding of historical and cultural trends." He had slipped into academic-speak.

"I don't think my 'differences' can be explained away so easily."

Professor McMaster sat back in his chair and folded his hands into a triangular shape. While he looked the part of a professor, I wondered whether he truly felt the role or was using it as a protective measure. After all, I'd just strolled in here and bandied about the skeleton in his closet. "Tell me about your"—he hesitated, and then picked the word—"differences."

"You witnessed one of my 'differences' just now. By touching people, I can read certain thoughts, those that are currently passing through their minds."

"Yes, that was—impressive. Can you extract people's thoughts by any other means?" he asked, very matter-of-factly.

I hesitated. Was it too risky to tell him? I had no alternative but to divulge my darkest secret to a stranger. "Yes, through their blood."

He did not seem fazed. Had he met others like me? Or just a slew of kooks pretending to be vampires? He continued with his line of questioning. "By touching or tasting their blood?"

I'd gone this far; I might as well disclose everything. "By tasting their blood."

Professor McMaster nodded and continued with his questions, as if processing my credentials. He was remarkably composed. "Do you possess any other special skills?"

"I can fly."

This alone seemed to surprise him. "You mean that you can actually take flight?"

"Yes."

"That is most unusual." He rose and started pacing around his little office. While he didn't appear frightened or repelled by my strangeness, he did seem thrown off. As if I'd messed up his categorization of otherworldly beings.

There was a knock on his door. He muttered something about his seminar students and excused himself. He unlocked the door, stepped outside, and closed the door behind him. I heard a muffled exchange. It sounded like Professor McMaster was trying to persuade his student to wait patiently for a few minutes.

He returned, closing the door tightly behind him. "Other than an understanding of your skills, do you have any

information about your nature or origins? Even an intuition of your identity might prove helpful."

"Just what my parents told me." I'd been reluctant
to mention my mom and dad. Because of what Ezekiel
said, I wanted to keep them as far out of this as possible.
But I had to share it; I didn't want to risk getting useless
information.

"Your parents know about your skills?" For good reason, he sounded shocked. What teenager would tell their
parents about that?

"Yes."

"What did they tell you?" His natural impatience surfaced.

"My father told me a Bible story, and told me it was relevant. It was from Genesis, and it dealt with angels, their
Nephilim creations, and Noah's flood."

Professor McMaster went to his shelves and plucked out
a well-worn copy of the Bible. He read aloud the verses
from Genesis that my dad told me about. Then he stared
at me. "Miss Faneuil, your parents didn't explain the rel-
evance of this biblical passage to you?"

"No." In fact, I had inferred from my parents' story that I
was some kind of angel. Particularly since God had ordered
the annihilation of all Nephilim.

"They just told you a story and let you draw your own
conclusions about your unusual powers?" He sounded

justifiably incredulous.

It did sound preposterous, particularly without the context of the full story my parents shared and their own identity as angels. But I had no intention of telling that to the professor. Obviously, I needed to divulge something more, or risk sounding ridiculous. So I offered him a fairly irrelevant tidbit, for my purposes anyway. "Well, they did say that the vampire legend emerged from the presence of these fallen angels in our world, once they had been cast out of heaven for creating the Nephilim."

He looked confused—but excited. "What did they tell you?"

I tried to clarify. "God insisted that these angels—the ones that mated with man—remain on earth as punishment, right? My parents explained that, from time to time, these fallen angels appeared at the side of a dying man or woman. For good and bad purposes. Occasionally, mankind witnessed these angels, and man fashioned the vampire myth around them."

Professor McMaster practically leapt from his seat. "Can you repeat that?"

I did the best I could. As I spoke, his eyes lit up, and he clapped his hands. "This is terribly exciting. It is a very interesting—indeed unique—explanation for the creation of the vampire myth. Even an explanation for the existence of vampires themselves."

Odd that he seemed more excited about uncovering the origins of a legend than he did about the possibility of finding a real live supernatural creature in his office. But I supposed there was no accounting for the eccentricities of academics.

He seemed to realize the idiosyncrasy of his behavior and backtracked by saying, "But of course, we need to focus on your question, Miss Faneuil. I confess to no great familiarity with Nephilim or biblical creatures, but we could talk further and do some investigation. And I have an acquaintance with a noted scholar in the field that we might contact."

"I would really appreciate that, Professor McMaster." I wondered if he was being so helpful because he feared my knowledge of Istvan Laszlof or because he wanted to hear more about the genesis of the vampire fable. It certainly wasn't due to any innate kindness.

Another knock rattled on his door. He rose and said, "We obviously need some uninterrupted time. Let me meet with some of these anxious students, and let us meet back in my office at five P.M. today. I will see what I can find out in the meantime."

Five o'clock sounded so far away. "Is there no way to meet sooner? I'm afraid there's some urgency to my question."

"No, Miss Faneuil. It would be impossible." His door shuddered with a knock—again. "Not without constant disruption."

My heart sank at the thought of waiting around until five.

Not so for Professor McMaster. His eyes lit up, and he said, "Later, you can tell me all about the beginnings of the vampire myth." Hardly my interest.

THIRTY-SEVEN

I walked out of Professor McMaster's building and into the sea of students that filled up Harvard Square. For a split second, I felt like one of them, caught up in the excitement of fresh discoveries and the frenzy of deadlines. I slung my bag across my chest, imagining it to be full of term papers instead of scribbles on the mysteries of myself, and pretended to be a student at the college of my dreams.

But then I saw a distinctive flash of short, white-blond hair across the square. My heart started racing and, even though my gut told me to run in the opposite direction, I followed it as it bobbed away from the square. I needed to know if that hair belonged to Ezekiel or Michael—and whether they had already found me. Plus, I told myself that it would be better to learn the truth while in a crowd. Safety in numbers and all that.

The person moved quickly, darting from one side street to the next in a mad dash somewhere. I tried to keep his pace while keeping my distance, but it wasn't easy; I was no trained detective. Just when I thought I'd hit my stride, he took an unexpected, sharp right turn down a more commercial road and disappeared from my sight. I craned my neck trying to get a look. Countless blond students walked down the road, but none had the distinctive platinum shimmer of Ezekiel or Michael. I slowed down, furious with myself for losing either one of them. If it was really Ezekiel or Michael.

The remnants of adrenaline coursed through me. I allowed the remaining momentum to carry me away from the commercial thoroughfare into the far reaches of the campus. The crowds thinned as the students raced into classes, and I found myself in a little brick courtyard bordered by ivy-covered walls. It was straight from a campus movie set, picture perfect—almost too perfect.

The spot looked so inviting. A wrought-iron bench sat in one corner, under a weeping willow tree. I hadn't slept the night before, and nothing in the world looked more enticing than that courtyard and that bench. I slowed my pace even more, strolled over to the bench, and sat down.

For the first few minutes, I just breathed in the calmness of the place and watched the students trickle into class. They reminded me of the feeling of belonging I'd experienced just before I'd glimpsed the possible Ezekiel or Michael, the brief fantasy I'd had about actually being a Harvard student. I realized that the fleeting playacting might be the closest I would ever come to being a college student. How could someone like me—whatever I was— hope to move past all this drama and strangeness and go to college?

I started crying. Pretty quickly, the trickle of tears turned into a torrent, and I was sobbing. All I wanted was a normal life—a high school boyfriend, a good college, supportive parents, and nice friends. Instead, here I was, a sixteen-year-old girl, totally on my own—no parents or friends that I could contact, and certainly no boyfriend to speak of— trying to figure out what I was.

Out of nowhere, a sweet-looking blond girl wearing a Harvard sweatshirt stood before me. She asked, "Are you all right? Can I get you anything?"

Through my tears, I answered. "No, I'm fine. Thanks for asking."

Before I could offer her a seat, she sat down beside me. She didn't actually touch me, but her presence felt comforting. Almost as if she'd hugged me.

"You know, when you are looking for answers, it is always best to start with the questions."

"Pardon me?" Her advice seemed an odd choice to offer a sobbing stranger on a college campus, even though her demeanor was otherwise soothing.

She laughed a delightful, tinkly-sounding giggle. "I'm sorry. My friends are always accusing me of being obscure. All I meant was that you look like you are struggling with some big issues. I always return to the questions when looking for answers to a tough problem. Then I start my research."

"I'm sure you're right."

The girl smiled serenely and then handed me a tissue. Abruptly, she stood up and said, "Well, I better run. I'm really late for class."

After wiping away the rest of my tears so I appeared somewhat presentable, I looked up to thank her. But the girl had disappeared into the thicket of sidewalks and buildings surrounding the courtyard.

Her words lingered, as did her pervading sense of calm. Maybe she was right. Maybe the answers lay in the questions themselves—in part, anyway. And maybe I should start researching the answers to those questions. After all, I was at Harvard, one of the research capitals of the world.

I stopped the pity party, and really homed in on my questions, the ones I'd scribbled down on the train ride. More than anything, I wanted to know who I was. I didn't know whether I was a fallen angel, one of these Nephilim beings, or some creature related to the biblical stories. But

I did know that I was important enough that two "good" fallen angels sacrificed their own immortality to raise me as their own daughter. I also knew that one of the "bad" fallen angels—Ezekiel—said that I was destined to rule at his side. I didn't think his words were mere flattery; given his advanced gifts, Ezekiel could lure any number of people to join his ranks without hyperbole. Whatever I was, the stakes were high. And I needed to find out, to deal with Ezekiel.

Only six hours left until I met Professor McMaster again. I would use the time to prepare—even arm myself—for the coming days.

I left my peaceful little courtyard with reluctance, even though I welcomed the safety of the student crowds. When I finally reached the throngs in Harvard Square, I felt like I'd been tossed a life preserver.

But then I saw that distinctive flash of platinum again. And I knew that evil lurked in the masses as well as on deserted streets. Ezekiel was here, and he was taunting me.

THIRTY-EIGHT

After consulting a guidebook, I decided to visit the Andover-Harvard Theological Library, on the northeast part of the campus. The guide described the library as containing a preeminent collection of biblical research materials, one of the largest in the United States. If I was going to find helpful information on angels or other biblical creatures, I guessed the Andover-Harvard Theological Library would be the place.

The directions from Harvard Square to the library were a little complicated, and I was more than a little distracted by any blond passersby. So it took me half an hour to get there, rather than the estimated fifteen minutes. I got more and more anxious with each step; the clock was ticking.

Finally, I spotted the stone gothic building described in the guide: Andover Hall. The hall connected to a building of more modern design, and the library nestled between the two. Following the map, I entered the hall through a center entrance under the gothic tower. I then started down a long hallway called the cloister walk, which was lined in old stones and what looked like discarded church pews.

At the very end of the cloister walk waited a closed door—the library entrance. I opened it with a deafening creak, and then busied myself with a lobby display while I waited for the circulation desk to become busy so I could sneak in. I had read that the library was used primarily by masters' and doctoral students and, while I might pass as a college freshman, posing as a graduate student was a major stretch.

After skirting past the circulation desk and racing up a flight of stairs, I headed into the Houghton Reference Room. I sat at a computer dedicated to searching the library collections, and placed my fingers on the keyboard. Where should I even begin? I typed in "fallen angels," but got thousands of hits. So I narrowed my search to the unusual word my dad mentioned: Nephilim.

A few matches flashed on the screen. Other than the Book of Genesis from the Bible—which I had expected—I saw entries for the Book of Enoch. What was that?

I quickly scribbled down the reference number for the Book of Enoch and headed into the stacks. Along the way, I grabbed a copy of the Bible—an easy matter in a theological library—so I could look at that Genesis quote again. But finding the Book of Enoch was another matter altogether.

The stacks were endless. And overwhelming. How would I ever find this crazy book and read it in my dwindling time?

I must have looked lost, because a nice, but seriously nerdy-looking, student approached me. "Do you need some help?"

I almost said no, but the passing of time nagged at me. I smiled at the bespectacled student, and said, "Thanks so much. I'm looking for a copy of the Book of Enoch. Do you have any idea where one might be?"

"All too well. Follow me."

Silently, he led me down two flights of stairs. We entered the labyrinth of a different, larger set of stacks. Following his lead, I turned right and left and right again. Until he came to dead halt. He reached up to a high shelf, plucked down a book, and handed it to me.

The guy knew the book's location so well that I figured he must know something about its content. So I thanked him and whispered, "You certainly seem familiar with the Book of Enoch."

"I better be. Apocryphal Gospels are my area of focus."

"Apocryphal Gospels?"

He looked at me a bit askance but answered cordially

enough. "Biblical books that were considered for inclusion in the Old or New Testament, but that never made it, never became part of the accepted canon. You're not a divinity student, are you?"

"No. Is it that obvious?"

"Just a little." He smiled.

I smiled back. "Can you tell me anything about this Book of Enoch?"

"Well, it's an apocryphal gospel that was written between 300 B.C. and the first century B.C. It is not part of the canon for most Christian churches, except the Ethiopian Christian Church. But many of the New Testament writers were familiar with it, and it is quoted in the New Testament Letter of Jude. These facts have given it some credence in certain experts' minds."

"What's it about?"

"It's about many things."

"Anything in particular?"

"The Book elaborates on a passage from Genesis that deals with angels and Noah's flood. It discusses the creation of the Nephilim, as they are sometimes called—half angel and half man—and their destruction at the hands of a very angry God. Some say that their destruction was the impetus for Noah's flood." He pointed to a carrel jam-packed with books nearby. "I'm sitting just over there. Once you've read it, I'd be happy to try to answer any questions you have."

After thanking him profusely, I sat down in an empty carrel not too far away. I opened up the Bible and read the section of Genesis that my father had summarized. Although the language was dense, it told basically the same story as my dad. I was just about to close the Bible up and open the Book of Enoch when I noticed a footnote at the end of the relevant Genesis section. It read, "The Nephilim were thought to have been a race of giants, whose superhuman strength was attributed to semi-divine origin. They were the legendary worthies of ancient mythology." That sounded eerily familiar.

Then I started on the Book of Enoch. Although most of the language was old-fashioned and really hard to follow, one line toward the beginning was very clear:

> *The fallen angels were in all two hundred, who descended . . . and these are the names of their leaders: Samyaza, Arakiba, Sariel, Rameel, Armaros, Kokabiel, Tamiel, Ramiel, Baraqijal, Azael, Daniel, Hananel, and Ezekiel.*

I froze at the sight of my parents' names—and Ezekiel's. This ancient biblical story was becoming more and more real.

Tearing my eyes away from the list of fallen angels, I turned back to the story. In time, I got its archaic rhythm and began to parse together its tale. The Book told of all the wrong things the fallen angels did, the fury of God at the angels' creation of the Nephilim, and God's decision to bind the fallen angels to earth until the day of judgment. It sounded like the story my dad had told me, just a lot longer and lot harder to comprehend.

Certain passages jumped out at me. For example, I kept noticing that the Book of Enoch sometimes called the fallen angels "Watchers." I remembered that my mom had called Michael's mom a "former watcher." Were Michael's parents fallen angels too?

But I still wasn't sure what I was. The Book of Enoch bolstered my parents' statements that I wasn't a fallen angel; after all, they were fixed in number and listed right there in the text. The book also rejected the notion that I was a Nephilim; they'd all been killed in Noah's flood from what I could tell. So the book hadn't answered my core question. Maybe there was a whole other category of biblical creatures that I'd overlooked.

I stopped by the carrel of the nice student who'd helped me. We chatted for a few minutes about the density of the ancient texts, and I thanked him again. I nearly reached the stairway when I thought of one last question and turned back.

"Assuming that the creatures described in the Bible really exist, would the Nephilim be around today? Or were they all killed in the flood?"

He paused for a moment, and then said, "Actually, at least one biblical expert maintains that a Nephilim will return at a critical point in mankind's existence—the end days."

"The end days?"

"Yeah, the end days—or Judgment Day, as the concept is sometimes called. They're a turbulent time preceding the return of a Messianic figure who'll judge all earthbound creatures and shepherd in a heavenly reign. All three of the Abrahamic religions—Christianity, Judaism, and Islam— contain this notion in some form." He talked as if he were reading from a textbook.

"And this expert thinks at least one Nephilim will emerge around these end days?"

"Yes. In fact, he believes the Nephilim is the creature referred to in the Book of Enoch as the 'Elect One.'"

Suddenly I remembered the predominance of that phrase throughout the book. And I also recalled one of the last lines of the Book of Enoch. It stated that the Elect One will lead at the end of time.

I felt goose bumps on my arms.

"Can you tell me the name of the expert who believes that the Nephilim will return?"

"Sure. His name is Professor Barr, and he's a professor of Biblical Studies at Oxford University in England."

Thirty-nine

The campus was growing dark, surprisingly dark for the time of day and the time of year. Almost as if the mere specter of Ezekiel cast a shadow on the whole of Harvard, blackening out any remaining daylight or the glow of the sunset. Or maybe it was just an illusion performed by Ezekiel for my benefit, like a storm cloud following me wherever I went.

As I approached Professor McMaster's building, I scanned it and determined that it was largely empty. Classes were over for the day, so I guessed the malingerers were stray students and obsessed professors. I found the same staircase I'd taken that morning and walked up the two flights to the professor's floor.

Pushing open the heavy staircase door, I stepped out into the darkened hallway. The secretaries' desk lights were off, and most of the professors' offices were closed for the day. The walk down the corridor to Professor McMaster's office seemed long, and I was relieved to see light peering out from under his closed door.

I knocked on the door, all too aware of the tangle of locks that lay on the other side and all too cognizant of the unpleasantness of my earlier greeting. I got no response.

The lights were on, but it was silent. I waited what seemed like an eternity. Had the professor had second thoughts?

Bracing myself to knock again, I finally heard the unfastening of locks accompanied by an unexpectedly cheerful reception: "Please come in, Miss Faneuil."

The door creaked open, and Professor McMaster's grinning face welcomed me in. His expression restored my hope. The thought fortified me. I smiled back and followed him inside.

But what I saw when I stepped inside wiped the smile off my face. In the battered wooden guest chair sat a man with white-blond hair and piercing blue eyes: Ezekiel.

No matter my horrified expression, Professor McMaster had smiles to spare. "Miss Faneuil, I have just been having the most intriguing conversation with your friend, Mister Ezekiel."

So, it was "my friend, Mister Ezekiel" now, was it? I had sensed him and Michael in Harvard Square, but I didn't expect to see him here. After all, he had instructed Michael

to wait until I came to them. Why I had any faith in the
assurances of evil itself, I don't know.

Ezekiel gave me his sickening smile. Using his most
polite tone, he said, "Hello, Ellspeth. We've been looking
forward to your arrival."

"I wish I could say the same."

Ezekiel ignored my snide remark, and the professor
seemed not to hear it at all. He was too fixated on Ezekiel,
who said, "I've been telling Professor McMaster all about
the interesting link between the fallen angels mentioned in
Genesis and the birth of the vampire mythology."

Turning away from Ezekiel in disgust and fear, I caught
a glimpse of the professor's face. His eyes positively shined
with excitement at the prospect of studying the true origins of the vampire legend and sharing his discovery with
the world; it would be the pinnacle of his life's work. At
that moment, I saw in the professor the same unquench-
able thirst for knowledge that I'd seen in the young Istvan
Laszlof's face, a thirst that caused him to take enormous
risks then with his life. And now, he was unwittingly risking his soul, as Ezekiel was determined to turn him toward
the darkness.

I stared over at Ezekiel, who smirked knowingly behind
the professor's back. He had no intention of ever allowing the professor to divulge the truth behind the vampire

legends; keeping the myth alive was one of his most useful weapons. But Ezekiel needed the professor, and he knew that this link between vampires and angels—paired with his formidable powers of persuasion—would sway Professor McMaster toward the darkness. And away from the light of helping me.

As I stood by helplessly, Ezekiel continued with his campaign to procure the professor.

"As I was saying, a most fascinating case presented itself in Tillinghast, Maine. One winter in the late 1800s, five of the fourteen children of a prominent farming family, the Stuckleys, suffered from tuberculosis. The family patriarch, Ezra, witnessed strange beings hovering around the first four of these five children on the eves of their deaths. So he watched over his pitiable fifth child, determined that these beings would not torment his sweet Honour. Unfortunately, one evening, he fell asleep during his vigil. He awoke to the horrific sight of a winged being drinking from the neck of his poor dying Honour—drinking her blood, that is. The creature fled when Ezra discovered him, but it was too late for Honour. You see, Professor, the creature was no vampire. It was one of the fallen angels I mentioned, called Daniel. But even angels have an insatiable thirst for blood. Hence, the legend."

I felt sick. My parents had mentioned an earlier visit

to Tillinghast. Could they have been involved in this Stuckley incident? I knew firsthand the powerful lure of blood. Or was Ezekiel just baiting me? More than likely, my parents had been there, trying to help bring the dying over to God.

As Professor McMaster listened to this nugget of history, his expression changed from mere excitement to utter devotion, and I knew Ezekiel had him. Watching as Ezekiel utilized his skills on the professor made me unexpectedly sympathetic to Michael. Ezekiel's talents were almost irresistible—to anyone but me, it seemed. Maybe Michael was more susceptible than I. Maybe his betrayal of me wasn't a matter of free will.

Witnessing this sick, soul-sucking process, a critical question formed in my mind. Why would Ezekiel go to all this trouble of turning the professor? Why wouldn't he just persuade me—or, better yet, force me—to join his ranks? Suddenly the words of the girl from the courtyard came to me, and I realized that the answer lay in the question itself. Ezekiel went to all this trouble because he couldn't force me to align with him. Unlike Michael, I had to choose Ezekiel.

This compelled Ezekiel to take desperate measures. He had to close down all avenues of escape—my parents and Ruth—and all pathways to information about my identity. He had to remind me constantly of his presence and power by using the tricks I witnessed over the past day. He had to leave me with one choice only: him.

Yet Ezekiel unwittingly tipped his hand through these actions. By trying to shut down my access to information about my nature, he told me just how important this information was to my salvation. Why else would he go to such lengths to keep it from me? For about the millionth time, I wished that my parents had told me everything.

But they hadn't. I would have to keep seeking out answers about my identity and purpose on my own— although I knew that Ezekiel would follow me wherever I went. Yet somehow, his actions didn't scare me off my quest—as he undoubtedly intended—but made me more determined than ever to embark on it. Even if it meant daring to use Ezekiel's own games against him to gain time and knowledge.

So I mustered up my courage and said, "Professor McMaster, Mr. Ezekiel, I'm so sorry to interrupt this captivating conversation. But I have to go."

"So soon?" Ezekiel asked with that ever-present sneer. As if he knew what I was up to.

"Unfortunately, yes." I turned to the professor. "Would you mind walking me to the door? It looks a bit like Fort Knox."

Professor McMaster tore his eyes away from Ezekiel

reluctantly and said, "Yes, yes, Miss Faneuil."

I followed the now-spellbound professor to the door. Although I could feel Ezekiel's eyes boring into my back, I didn't risk a final glance at him.

But Ezekiel wouldn't let me leave without a good-bye. And more. "Farewell, Ellspeth. Give my best to Hananel and Daniel. If you risk a visit home, that is."

I needed to get out of that room. I could feel the tentacles of Ezekiel's evil start to wrap around me.

Slowly, so slowly I thought I would scream, the professor painstakingly undid each lock. When he finished, I touched him on the hand, seemingly out of gratitude. As I did, I looked at him directly in the eyes, and willed him to forget about any information he might have gathered for me. Particularly anything he might know about this Professor Barr from Oxford that the Harvard student had mentioned. I prayed that the professor hadn't told Ezekiel anything already.

I said, "Thank you so much for your help, Professor McMaster. It's unfortunate that you didn't know more about my situation. Or anyone who could assist me."

When Professor McMaster answered, his voice sounded dazed from Ezekiel's efforts. "Yes, it is unfortunate, Miss Faneuil. But you are a smart young woman, and I am certain you will find your way."

Brushing up against his hand one last time, I scanned his thoughts and saw that the professor's mind was curiously blank. Had Ezekiel wiped it clean? Had I?

Racing down the hall away from the horror of Ezekiel, I heard Professor McMaster close his office door and then bolt all his locks. I wondered why he bothered. The professor had installed all those locks to keep out the malevolent creatures he studied, but now he had locked himself in with evil itself.

FORTY

I ran as fast as I could down the two flights of stairs to the building's exit. Only fear of detection by the remaining students or teachers prevented me from actually flying down. Once I reached the main floor, I thrust open the heavy wooden doors and breathed the cold nighttime air, as if I'd been saved from drowning.

The evening sky had turned from dark to pitch-black. The neighboring buildings and businesses had closed, eliminating a major source of light. I couldn't see a streetlamp anywhere. Even with my unusually sharp eyesight, I found the odd, shadowy landscape hard to make out.

Still, I was pretty sure of the route back to Harvard Square, where I could pick up the T to Logan Airport. It seemed that my next step must be meeting with this Professor Barr in London. I didn't think I could just phone the scholar up and ask my questions without being considered a kook or a crank. Anyway, where else could I go?

If my experiment had worked on Professor McMaster, I needed to take advantage of my small lead on Ezekiel and get the next flight to London. I had checked the schedule already and knew that a British Airways flight took off at eight P.M. If I really hustled, I might make it.

I followed a serpentine pathway leading away from the professor's building, then made a sharp left and right. By my calculations, I should have spotted Harvard Square in the distance, but I didn't. Instead, I found myself in a quadrangle of nearly deserted science buildings. I backtracked a little and tried out another right turn I'd considered. It led me right back to that science quadrangle. How could I be so lost? Desperate, I asked one of the few students I passed, and then diligently followed her directions. But I found myself in the science quadrangle once again. Was this another of Ezekiel's games? Or just another unfortunate turn of events in my nightmarish life?

I heard footsteps behind me, but didn't make much of them at first. Then I started to notice that the footsteps were matching my stride. So I took an unexpected sharp left turn as a test. The person followed.

I was scared. What if it was Ezekiel or Michael? I could handle pretty much anyone else. I pivoted and started running in the other direction. I could hear the person gaining on me. I had no choice. I had to fly.

Almost instantaneously, my back expanded, and my body streamlined for flight. My feet had just started to levitate, when I felt a hand pull at my foot. I struggled to kick it off, but the person was strong. I fell down to the ground on top of my pursuer.

"Ellie, it's me. It's Michael," he said, as if that was supposed to be a comfort.

I shoved away his outstretched hand, and pushed myself off him and onto the hard concrete of the pathway. "I can see that. Why would I want to see you?"

"You have every right to be furious with me, Ellie. But it's me—the real Michael." He looked at me with those familiar green eyes, and it did seem as though my Michael stared out through them. But how could I be sure?

"I thought I went to Ransom Beach with the real Michael. But unfortunately, it was Ezekiel's underling."

Very, very gently, he reached for me. Even though it seemed a gesture of comfort, I pulled away. It would take a lot more convincing before I'd let him touch me. "I understand, Ellie. I didn't like what I became either. Do you know how scary it is to watch yourself say and do things you'd never imagine, and be unable to stop?"

From witnessing the transformation of Professor McMaster, I knew that Michael's words were entirely possible. I wanted it to be true. But I still didn't trust him. After all, he'd seemed like my Michael when we flew down the cliff to Ransom Beach—right into Ezekiel's waiting arms. Ezekiel must have turned him the night before.

I crossed my arms, and gave him a thorough once-over. No glazed eyes, no deadened speech, but still, I wasn't certain. "How did you change back to yourself?"

"Last night, your parents came over to my house—to talk to my parents. It was really late, and they didn't know I was still awake. So I eavesdropped on them. For some reason, hearing them talk about you snapped the connection between me and Ezekiel."

I wanted to know what my parents had said, but assessing Michael's truthfulness was far more critical just now.

"If you aren't aligned with Ezekiel anymore, why are you here in Boston with him?" I asked the obvious question.

"I knew Ezekiel would find you. So I snuck out of the house and called to him—pretending that I was still in his sway. Though it was quite a trick making sure I didn't come into physical contact with him, so he wouldn't discover the truth. He kept saying we should hold off until you reached out to us, but I knew that he'd try to find you. He just couldn't stay away from you."

"Why aren't you with him right now?"

"I knew Ezekiel wanted to meet with that professor you

found—to find out what he knew and what he told you. When he went into the professor's office, I told him that I would meet him outside afterward; Ezekiel didn't want me in there anyway. That was my opportunity to break from him and track you down."

"Why did he let me leave the professor's office?"

"Ezekiel probably wanted to finish what he started—either getting information from the professor or turning him into one of his minions. I think he liked the irony of having a vampire scholar in his ranks. Anyway, he can find us again whenever he wants us."

"How does he track us?" This question figured prominently on my big list. I needed to know how Ezekiel could find me, so I could figure out to hide from him.

"Once I started using my powers, I became like a blip on a radar screen to him, as he described it. He and I are somehow linked through our blood. That's what he told me, anyway."

Michael had only answered one-half of my question—the part about him. "But that doesn't explain how he tracks me."

He averted his eyes before responding. "You have my blood in your veins. So he can track you, too."

I felt sick. There was nowhere to hide from Ezekiel because I'd tasted Michael's blood and now it ran in my veins? No wonder Michael didn't want to look me in the face when he delivered that piece of news. "Great."

Michael paused and then pleaded with me. "Please, Ellie. Give me another chance."

I hesitated. I wanted to believe Michael, and it sickened me to think that Ezekiel had put him up to this little reunion. I didn't want to go on this crazy, scary journey all by myself. But after everything I'd been through, I couldn't believe him. Not without proof.

I tightened my crossed arms. "How can I be sure you're telling the truth, Michael?"

"There is only one way to know for certain," he said.

Michael was right. There was only one way.

This was no gentle kiss. This was no soft exchange of tongue and teeth. Michael didn't deserve any tenderness or affection. I was mad at him for his betrayal, whether or not it was consciously done. I leaned over and bit him. Hard. Like a vampire.

FORTY-ONE

Michael's blood rushed into my mouth. I staggered from the force of its flow and the power of its images. I'd never known his blood to have such strength, but then I'd never procured it by violent means before.

Looking through Michael's eyes, I stood on the second floor landing of his house. A tall, elegantly curved grandfather clock stood next to me, and its hands met at twelve. I peered down the curved staircase and caught the tiniest glimpse of my parents and his parents in the entryway. They were talking in hushed tones—presumably so as not to awaken Michael—but I could hear them if I strained and ignored the ticking. Interestingly, though, the scene looked filmy, as if Michael's vision was hazy.

"What is it, Hananel? You look distraught," Michael's mom asked.

"Ellspeth is gone." My own eyes welled up with tears at the despair in my usually unflappable mother's voice.

"What do you mean 'gone'?" She sounded alarmed.

"I mean that she was supposed to be home by five, after she had coffee with her friend, Ruth. I'd given Ellspeth a special exemption from her grounding to meet with Ruth, since their friendship had been strained lately—" My mom's voice broke, and I saw my dad put his arm around her shoulder as she cried.

"It's all right, Hananel. What happened?" Michael's mom prompted her.

"Ellspeth didn't come home. I waited until six to contact Ruth, who claimed to be confused because she had dropped Ellspeth at our house. But Daniel and I didn't believe her, so we asked Ruth to come over. She was visibly nervous when she arrived; obviously she knew something. At first, she clung to her original story that she had brought Ellspeth home. We used the vestiges of our skills to find out more, but all Ruth knew was that Ellspeth had had some kind of fight with Michael. So, at Ellspeth's insistence, Ruth took her to the train station. Ruth didn't know where Ellspeth planned to go." Silently, I cheered on Ruth for keeping quiet about the flying. Even though my parents already knew about it, of course.

"But you're afraid that it's more than a teenage fight? You think that she left for other reasons?" Michael's mom asked.

"Yes, Sariel," my dad answered. "We talked to Ellspeth

last night. We read her the passage about the Nephilim and—"

"What?" Michael's dad practically yelled.

"Keep your voice down, Armaros," Michael's mom warned. Sariel? Armaros? Hadn't I seen those names in the Book of Enoch? Michael's parents must be "good" fallen angels too, as I'd suspected.

"You didn't tell her who she is, did you?" Armaros asked, his voice incredulous.

"Don't be ridiculous. Her ignorance is the only thing that has protected her so far. The same goes for Michael. You know that," my dad said. He was as angry as I'd ever heard him.

"Then why would you come so dangerously close to revealing the truth to her?"

"Her powers have started to emerge. The poor thing thought she was a vampire. We needed to give her just enough information to dissuade her of that misconception—and explaining the link between the fallen angels and vampires was the only way. We didn't tell her anything more." I knew that this last point wasn't exactly true, but I was glad Armaros didn't. He was fierce.

"Daniel, how could you be so foolish? We were meant to protect them longer, keep them unaware until they were ready. Until it was time." Armaros continued sparring with my dad.

"What were our choices, Armaros? To let her go on believing she was a vampire? And have Michael believe the same thing too? Such thinking would bring them precariously close to darkness. When Ezekiel or the others emerge, as they undoubtedly will, it would make Ellspeth and Michael easy prey for their dark purposes."

I felt something snap in Michael, almost like he'd woken up. And suddenly I saw the image more clearly, not through some bizarre haze. I guessed that the haze was the residue of Ezekiel's influence.

"You're right, Daniel. But while it is one thing for Ellspeth to be aware of her differences, it is quite another for her to even suspect who she is. You may have opened the door just enough to put Ellspeth and Michael in play, assuming Ellspeth told him what she knows," Armarmos barked back at my dad. Then he said quietly, "You might have even triggered the end days."

"You don't think I know that, Armaros? Hananel and I tried so hard to make Ellspeth feel like a regular human— to align her with mankind when it's time and to stave off her powers and the clock. You don't think I've worried myself sick over when to tell her who she is? When to begin preparing her for the battle that rages beneath the surface in this naive world? We have walked a very fine line between keeping her safe and innocent and preparing her for war. How can we possibly know the best course for Ellspeth and Michael when we haven't seen their kind since—"

Armaros interrupted. With venom. "Since the beginning."

"Enough fighting," my mom interjected. "We don't know that either Ellspeth or Michael know anything of significance. We do know that Ellspeth is gone, and we need to find her. We have sent a gifted friend to track her down and bring her home, since obviously we cannot go ourselves—"

"Obviously," Michael's mom interrupted.

"And we were hoping that you might send one of your friends to do the same," my mom finished.

"We would be happy to do so, Hananel." Michael's mom paused and then said, "Thank goodness, Michael doesn't know anything."

"Nothing?" My mom sounded skeptical.

"He senses his powers, of course. But, otherwise, he seemed perfectly normal at dinner tonight. If a little subdued."

"He didn't mention a fight with Ellspeth?"

"No. But then, you know how teenagers are."

"Are you certain that he is uninformed?"

"Insofar as I can be certain of anything with the limitations of this mortal body."

"Perhaps you should check on him."

"Perhaps I should."

The stairs began to creak as Sariel walked up to Michael's bedroom. I watched through his eyes as he scurried back to his bedroom and threw himself under the covers. The wooden floorboards squeaked as she approached his bed and hovered over it for several minutes. Then she tiptoed out of the room, closing the door behind her.

The image faded. I stood before Michael, staring into his waiting eyes. He looked almost sick as he anticipated my judgment on the image he had summoned up for me.

"Do you believe me? Do you believe that Ezekiel doesn't have a hold on me any longer?"

I did. I knew he was telling the truth. In fact, I sensed the very moment when the cord between Michael and Ezekiel was cut—it was when my dad mentioned Ezekiel by name—and I knew that Michael came to Boston of his own volition. Not under Ezekiel's sway or for Ezekiel's purposes.

"I do, Michael."

"Thank God."

Michael wrapped his arms around me, and I let him. I

didn't return the embrace. I wasn't ready. But I couldn't stay mad at him either. Through Ezekiel's eyes, I'd seen Ezekiel turn powerful, grown men and women into his followers. Into monsters. How did I expect Michael to resist?

"Ellie, I promise that I will never betray you again. We're in this together, against Ezekiel."

"I hope so, Michael." I really did. But how could I be certain that Michael wouldn't fall under Ezekiel's influence again? I knew Ezekiel would be a constant presence, in one form or another, and Michael seemed to be susceptible to Ezekiel in a way that I wasn't. I would have to be vigilant, to constantly assess Michael for any changes, by touch or by blood if necessary.

But for now, it was enough that Michael was back. And that I was no longer entirely alone.

FORTY-TWO

Hand in hand, we raced across the Harvard campus toward the square. The lights from the stores and restaurants and theater blinded my sensitive eyes after the dimness of the campus pathways. In the few seconds it took for them to adjust, Michael led me down into the murky tunnels of the T; the strange disorientation I'd experienced on the Harvard campus must have been an Ezekiel trick. I bristled at the thought of being underground—trapped—but with Ezekiel so near, we had no choice.

I had told Michael where we needed to go and how fast we needed to get there. To his credit, he didn't ask why. He just asked how he could help us reach Professor Barr.

At Michael's suggestion, I had tried to reach Professor Barr by phone first, without success. The time difference was working against us, so we decided the quickest—and perhaps only—way to reach him under the circumstances was to fly to London.

After quickly mapping out the necessary connections to get from the Harvard Square Station to Logan Airport, we stood on the train platform. Using Michael's cell, we booked seats on the British Airways flight to London. And then we waited. An ancient clock loomed over our heads and tapped out the minutes, as if reminding us how little time we had before the gate would close. I wished that we ourselves could fly to London, but neither of us knew whether we had the ability to fly such far distances.

Finally, finally, in the far distance, I heard the rumbling of the train. I thanked God. I didn't think my nerves could stand one more second of delay. One more second for Ezekiel to find us.

The crowds started to converge on the cramped platform as the train slowed down. As the doors opened, people jostled for spots in the already packed train car. I reached for Michael's hand to make sure we didn't lose each other. Before his hand gripped mine, I saw a familiar head of blond hair in the crowd pouring into the train.

I stopped. Was it Ezekiel?

I felt the warmth of Michael's hand in mine, and yet I still couldn't move. The man looked like he was about to hop on board, but was hesitating. Should we stay here— and risk missing our flight—or get on an enclosed subway car with Ezekiel for company?

Michael pulled me toward the open train doors. They had started to beep in anticipation of closing. "Come on, Ellie. The doors are about to shut."

My body was rigid. Michael spun around and saw my expression. He followed my gaze and understood immediately the source of my fear.

"Ellie, it's not Ezekiel."

The man was facing the other way, so I couldn't see his features. But his hair so resembled Ezekiel's distinctive color and style, I didn't trust Michael. "How do you know?"

Rather than wasting precious time explaining, Michael released my hand, ran over to the man, and tapped him on the shoulder. When the man turned around, I saw the ruddy face of a young college student. Not Ezekiel.

Just before the doors slid shut, Michael dragged me on board. College students jammed the car, so we clutched onto the metal rings for support as the train lurched forward. I exhaled in relief and willed my heart to stop racing.

At the next stop, the Central Square Station, most of the students got off. A bench opened up. We grabbed it and settled in for the fifteen-minute ride to South Station, where we'd transfer to the bus for Logan.

We rode in silence. I became acutely aware of all that we hadn't talked about: the overheard conversations of our parents, my discussions with Professor McMaster,

Michael's time alone with Ezekiel. The unspoken words hung between us, like a screen separating us. I didn't want to feel so detached from Michael, but I didn't know where to start. Or how to break through the divide.

Finally, Michael tried. He looked at me, with a serious and sad expression, and asked, "Ellie, what are we?"

I hesitated. I wasn't certain of my conclusion at all, but he deserved to know the most logical assumption. "I think we're something called Nephilim. But I'm not really sure what that means."

Michael's lips formed the first of many questions, but my eyes suddenly grew heavy. I hadn't slept for nearly two days. He whispered, "It's all right, Ellie. Go to sleep. We have plenty of time to figure this all out. I'll stay awake so we don't miss our stop."

His arms enfolded me, and I returned the gesture. I hadn't hugged him since he returned to himself. And it felt good.

For the first time since I met Michael on Ransom Beach, I relaxed and closed my eyes. His arms and his reassurances that we would uncover the mysteries of our beings together soothed me. I wanted to thank him, so I forced my eyes open a little.

My drowsy vision settled on a sweet-faced blond girl wearing a Harvard sweatshirt walking down the train car aisle. She resembled the helpful girl from the peaceful brick courtyard, the one who advised me to think about the questions. I thought she smiled at me. I started to smile back, but then a disturbing question crossed my mind. It wiped away all thoughts of sleep. With all the thousands of college students in Cambridge, what were the odds that I'd run into the same person twice within a few hours? Slim, very slim.

FORTY-THREE

My eyes flew open, and I looked at her a little closer. It was the girl from the Harvard courtyard. It couldn't be a coincidence.

I nudged Michael to watch the girl as she continued down the aisle in our direction. The train hurtled down the tracks, plunging the car deeper and deeper into the warren of underground T tunnels and making any immediate escape impossible. But the girl seemed impervious to the jolting of the train; she just walked serenely toward us.

As she approached our seat, the older man on the bench facing us got up. Even though the train hadn't slowed and we were nowhere near a station. She settled into the vacated seat and beamed that sweet smile at me.

"Hello, Ellspeth."

I didn't think I'd told her my name during our brief discussion in the courtyard. And I certainly wouldn't have called myself Ellspeth even if I had. "How do you know my name?"

"Your parents sent me." From the conversation Michael had overheard, I knew that my parents had mentioned sending a "friend" to watch over me. But how did I know she wasn't a "friend" of Ezekiel's instead?

As if she knew I needed reassurance, the girl said, "Your mother asked me to give you this, as a sign of my loyalty to you. And to Michael, of course." Although she referred to Michael as if he was an afterthought.

She put an object in my hand, and then closed my fist around it. I opened my fingers one by one, and discovered my mother's locket inside. I had never seen my mom without it. How had this girl gotten it from her? I guessed she could have taken it from my mom by force, even though my intuition told me otherwise.

To answer my unspoken question, the girl placed her hand over mine. I received a precise, vivid flash, as if she explicitly sent the image to me. It was a very different sensation than retrieving information from people's minds.

In the image, my mom and the girl stood in the entry-way of our house. My mom unfastened her locket and gingerly placed it in the girl's waiting palm.

"Take care of Ellspeth for me, and bring her home.

Give her this for me if she resists your good intentions." My mom smiled, and continued. "And knowing my strong-willed daughter, she may well resist."

"I will, Hananel."

The girl turned to leave, but my mom grabbed her by the arm before she went out the door. My mom gazed into the girl's eyes, as if she was speaking through them to me. "Please make Ellspeth understand that, by not rushing to her side, I'm not abandoning her. I'm trying to help her. And please tell her that there were reasons—vital reasons—why we didn't tell her who she is, or prepare her for what's to come."

"I promise, Hananel."

The image faded. I found myself back in the train car, clutching on to Michael's arm and staring into the face of an angel. For surely that is what she was. Her face had the same exquisite, timeless quality as did my parents. Or as my parents used to have, anyway.

I placed the locket around my neck. Sensing that her message was successfully received, the girl stretched out her hand to me. "Please come with me. We will get off at the next stop and fly somewhere safe."

I looked to Michael for agreement. He gave me a quick

nod, so I took her hand and stood up. As did Michael. "Who are you?" I asked.

"I am Tamiel," she answered as we started walking through the car. "I am also one of the fallen, trying for grace. Like both sets of your parents."

We followed Tamiel to the closed train doors. As we listened to the train hurtle down the tracks, I whispered, "I have so many questions."

She smiled that sweet, calming smile I'd seen in the Harvard courtyard. "I know, Ellspeth. I sensed that when we met earlier. So I guided you to a place where you could have certain questions answered without any harm befalling you. But I was tasked to bring you to safety. Not to illuminate you fully. It isn't time yet."

"Please, Tamiel. What are we?"

A crash sounded in the adjoining car, and we all jumped. Tamiel grabbed our arms and said, "We need to get out of here."

"Why?"

"Someone is coming for you."

"Ezekiel?" I asked.

Tamiel stopped and spun around. "How did you know that? I just discovered today that he had surfaced."

So our parents didn't know about the Ezekiel factor

yet. I was kind of glad they'd been spared that considerable worry. Especially since they didn't have any internal weaponry left with which to fight him. "He's been in contact with us."

"Yes, it's Ezekiel. And I don't think he will show any mercy."

"I don't think he'll hurt me, Tamiel."

Her bright blue eyes widened in astonishment. "Why do you say that?"

"I just sensed it. For some reason, I think Ezekiel needs me. I think he needs me to choose him."

"Well, you're right. But there are many ways to make you choose him. Especially since you care about mankind."

"Like?"

"Like threatening Michael, who is susceptible to his call. Like holding this entire train of innocent people hostage, until you come to his side." Her expression no longer appeared surprised, but angry at my delay. "Should I continue?"

"No." I remembered all too well the horrors I had seen through Ezekiel's eyes, and shuddered at the thought of being the reason for him to inflict more suffering on others.

"Then let's go." We linked hands and exited our train car. I felt the warm rush of the underground air, as the doors closed behind us and we stepped onto the rickety outdoor platform connecting the two train cars.

Tamiel crossed over first, holding on to my hand the entire time. I hesitantly stepped over the divide, when I heard a huge thud in the train car we'd just left.

"I hope we aren't too late," Tamiel said, as she pulled me and Michael over to the other side. And we ran into the next car.

Forty-four

The train car was packed. With Tamiel in the lead, we pushed and elbowed our way through the crowd to reach the next set of doors. But not before we heard a deafening smash on the opposite side of the car.

"Don't turn around," Tamiel yelled, and shoved me and Michael through the doors onto the connecting platform.

She propelled us into the next car and the next, staying at our backs as a shield against an obviously angry Ezekiel. As we raced through the speeding train, we heard thuds and crashes in our wake. But we couldn't stop to look or speculate; we had to keep moving. Even when we heard screams from other passengers.

We reached the doors of the last car. I wondered what Tamiel had planned, as the sounds of Ezekiel's rampage hadn't stopped. In fact, they had only increased. And I knew enough to be terrified.

Tamiel pried the last set of train doors open, and pushed

us onto the platform. It swerved back and forth as the train sped down the track, and I didn't think we'd be able to keep our footing. But then, I realized that Tamiel didn't intend for us to use our feet at all.

We linked hands, and our bodies geared up for flight. I felt my shoulders broaden and the familiar warmth spread across them. I looked over at Michael to see if he was prepared. He nodded at me, and I squeezed his hand in reply. I was ready—as ready as I'd ever be to fly down the treacherous, underground tunnels of the T.

Just as our feet began to lift, the platform shook violently. I nearly fell off, but Tamiel pulled me back before I tumbled down onto the electrified tracks. As I steadied myself so we could take off, I said a silent word of thanks to my mom for sending Tamiel, and looked over at her in gratitude for saving me.

But then I felt the earth shift hard under the tracks, and I screamed. Ezekiel was standing right next to Tamiel.

In the split second that Tamiel spun around to look at him, I second-guessed her. Perhaps the locket and the image of my mom and the chase through the train were just part of a trap to lead us to Ezekiel. But then I saw the expression on her face—a mix of astonishment and fear— and I knew that I was wrong. She was on our side.

The only one smiling was Ezekiel.

"That scream was not much of a welcome, Ellspeth. And here I've been searching everywhere for you and Michael."

Ezekiel reached for me, and I recoiled. I started backing up. Flight was the only way I could escape him, but my body wasn't prepared yet. Just as his fingers grazed my arm, I felt Tamiel swoop me up into the air.

Within moments, I was able to soar on my own, and follow Tamiel down the warm, dank tunnels. The space was disorienting and narrow, so narrow that my arm brushed against a slimy tile wall. I reminded myself of the torture I'd seen in Ezekiel's vision—torture that would be visited upon me, and God knew who else, if he caught us. So I held my tongue and flew.

As Tamiel raced down the passageways, Michael and I flanked her as best we could. She was incredibly fast and made sharp turns down the labyrinthine passageways of the T as if she'd memorized the entire system. Maybe she had; maybe she knew it would come to this.

The wall tiles turned from red to green signaling the switch in train lines, and we veered left down a tight tunnel. I felt a sudden whoosh behind me, and I pivoted in midair to see what caused it. Ezekiel's shiny hair and pale face loomed in the distance.

"He's gaining on us," I called up to Tamiel.

She didn't respond. Instead she sped up and made a

quick, unexpected right turn. Michael and I raced to follow her. A roar and a blinding light greeted us in the mouth of the tunnel she'd just entered. We found ourselves facing an oncoming train.

Michael and I nearly spun back around—into the advancing arms of Ezekiel—but we saw Tamiel propel herself up and over the moving train. Mirroring her actions, we trailed her as she shot straight up through a tiny shaft in the ceiling of the tunnel.

The shaft was so constricted that Michael and I could barely fit through the opening. But once we squeezed ourselves through, it broadened, allowing us to regain speed. We followed Tamiel through the pitch-blackness as she climbed upward to the surface.

The air grew colder, and a glimmer of light appeared above us. Within seconds, Tamiel shoved aside a metal grate covering the shaft and peered upward. She motioned for us to follow her as she flew up and out.

We stood at the far, dark corner of a T stop—Government Center. A train must have just left, because the stop was mercifully empty. Without a word of explanation, Tamiel sprinted down the long platform toward the exit, and we chased after her. After tearing up two flights of stairs, we stood outside in the frigid nighttime of downtown Boston. The fresh air was a relief after the fetid underground, but I was reluctant to trade flying for running. I felt like I could hold my own a bit better against Ezekiel if I flew.

We could see and hear the lights and noise of the nearby tourist attraction Faneuil Hall. I assumed that we'd head in the opposite direction, and started walking the other way. But Tamiel pulled me toward Faneuil Hall instead.

"I thought you wanted us to stay away from crowds. You said that Ezekiel could use them as a weapon against us," I said, as we began running toward the busy eighteenth-century marketplace built around a cobblestone promenade where street performers entertained tourists while they shopped and ate.

"He can. But the crowds also limit his powers and provide us with a means of escape."

"Why is he doing this, Tamiel? He's had the chance to take us by force before, but he never tried."

"He's furious with Michael for deceiving him outside Professor McMaster's office, to start. And—" Tamiel stopped herself. As if she'd said too much already.

"Tell me, Tamiel."

"He believes that you are dangerously close to understanding who you are. Once you fully comprehend your nature and purpose, the end days will begin. And Ezekiel can no longer wait. He will want you at his side."

FORTY-FIVE

I sensed—rather than saw or heard—Ezekiel following us toward Faneuil Hall. I knew that Michael and Tamiel did too because each time my instinct told me to veer left or right to avoid him, they did the same—without speaking.

We moved like this—in unison—and entered Faneuil Hall. Despite the cold, the place was packed. We weaved through vendors hawking wares and tourists sipping hot drinks and jugglers entertaining them. Tamiel was right; the crowds provided a shield for us and compromised Ezekiel's ability to lash out. For the moment.

After several minutes hurrying through the crowds as a unit, Tamiel suddenly broke and took the lead. She led us into an impressive building with huge colonnades and a brass sign that read QUINCY MARKET. Inside was an enormous indoor food court, jammed with tables, stalls, and even more people.

Cutting through the crowds like a knife, Tamiel headed straight for the doors at the rear. Clearly she had brought us into Quincy Market only as a diversion and a way to shake Ezekiel. Michael and I kept her pace and followed her to the far end of the marketplace. I was so happy when I finally saw the exit doors next to a small stage.

Just as Tamiel reached for the door handle, I heard a loud slam reverberate throughout the busy hall. We spun around. All the doors to Quincy Market had simultaneously shut and locked. But the people continued eating and drinking and chatting as if nothing had happened.

We turned back toward the exit doors. There, on the stage, stood Ezekiel. It was the scenario I most feared.

Ezekiel pasted on that sickening smile of his and started pacing the stage. He stared at us, but spoke to Tamiel in a triumphant voice. "I am going to tell them who they are."

"Please don't, Ezekiel." I heard begging from the seemingly invincible Tamiel, and it terrified me. I looked over at Michael, but he didn't meet my gaze. He was transfixed, watching the showdown between two angels.

"Does it scare you to think of them knowing the full story, Tamiel? Oh, I forgot. You would rather they learn the pretty little bits and pieces that you and the others feed them in sanitized places like the Harvard libraries."

"Have you no care for what will happen if you tell them everything?"

"Do you mean what might happen to you, Tamiel? And

the other fallen?" He gestured around the room. The people were oblivious to us; he must have used some trick to cloud us from their view. "Or do you mean what might happen to all of them? Oh, I was all for keeping Michael and Ellspeth in the dark at first, but now they probably know enough to start the clock. So I would like to be the one to share the entire story—instead of the watered-down versions those simpering fools who call themselves their parents will tell them. Michael and Ellspeth should know the truth and the role they are destined to play at the end."

Her voice became a thunderous clap. "Stop, Ezekiel!"

But her voice was no match for the roar of his own. He yelled back, "You will let them listen! Or I will set this place into a conflagration that matches hell's own fire. And that will only be the beginning."

Tamiel stayed where she was, but she withdrew from the fight. Ezekiel's voice quieted and took on that lulling tone that he seemed to find effective for his purposes. Then he met our eyes for the first time since we saw him in Quincy Market.

"Michael and Ellspeth, I have hoped to find you for a long, long time. Ever since that day when He"—Ezekiel spat out the word like a curse—"destroyed your fellow Nephilim, your brothers and sisters, in Noah's flood. From the very moment I learned about your conceptions, I've been looking for you. The people who claim to be your parents made my search difficult, surrendering their immortality so that your presences would be dark to me. They shrouded you in humanity that made you hard to find. But I finally found you, when your own powers surfaced. You became like a beacon to me. Or Michael did, at least. And through him, you, Ellspeth."

Ezekiel then asked, "Shall I tell you why I have longed for you?"

Michael and I didn't reply. How could you react when evil itself told you that you are the answer to its prayers?

"The key lies—in part—in the Book of Enoch." He smirked, and said, "Ellspeth, I believe you uncovered that during your little research today.

> *"When the congregation of the righteous shall appear,*
> *And sinners shall be judged for their sins,*
> *And shall be driven from the face of the earth;*
>
> *And when the Elect One shall appear before the eyes of the righteous,*
> *Whose elect works hang upon the Lord of the Spirits,*

*And light shall appear to the righteous and elect who dwell
on the earth. . . .*

*From that time those that possess the earth shall no longer be
powerful and exalted;*

*And they shall not be able to behold the face of the holy,
For the Lord of the Spirits has caused his light to appear
On the face of the holy, righteous, and elect.*

*Then shall the kings and the mighty perish
And be given into the hands of the righteous and holy.*

*And thenceforth none shall seek for themselves mercy from
the Lord of Spirits
For their life is at an end.*

"Do you know what that means?"

Michael and I had absolutely no idea, and Tamiel hadn't
uttered a word since Ezekiel had shut her up with the
threat of fire.

"No?" Ezekiel said with a smile. "Let me explain.
Ellspeth, I believe that Hananel and Daniel told you
that God cursed certain of us angels when we descended

to earth and created a race of our own by mating with humankind; that race was called the Nephilim. God—in His infinite hubris—was so furious at our act of creation that He wiped out all humans, save for his pet Noah and his kin. God then prohibited angels from procreation and banished us from heaven, leaving us here on earth as the so-called fallen. Did Hananel and Daniel tell you of this, Ellspeth?"

I nodded.

"The Book of Enoch describes how the fallen angels—like me and like your parents and even like Tamiel over there—will rule mankind until the end of time. Then, at the end, a select being will emerge whose purpose will be to judge the fallen angels and mankind. That select being—who Enoch calls the Elect One—is a Nephilim, part man and part angel." He smiled. "So you see, Enoch tells us that, regardless of God's specific command that the angels not procreate, the Nephilim will indeed come again. And one of those Nephilim will decide the fate of all beings on earth—angels and humans."

I felt sick. Suddenly, I knew where Ezekiel's story was going. He stretched out his hands toward me and Michael. "You are those Nephilim. And one of you is the Elect One."

FORTY-SIX

Come on. I had gotten used to the fact that I was different, something other than human. But this? Ezekiel expected me and Michael to believe that one of us was a chosen being, here to judge all creatures on earth at the end of time.

I shot Michael a look, but he seemed mesmerized once again. So I glanced over at Tamiel to gauge her reaction. She looked defeated. She also looked as deadly serious as Ezekiel.

"How does this explain why I have longed for your births? For centuries, even millennia?" Ezekiel said as he paced back and forth across the stage, lecturing to his captive audience.

He continued. "I knew that, once I found you, and the Elect One stood at my side, the fallen would be judged fairly at the end. For when the Elect One has learned what I have learned and has seen what I have seen, the Elect One would understand that the fallen are not sinners, but indeed the 'righteous and elect,' as Enoch said. And the fallen would continue to possess the earth—maybe even the heavens again."

It all became clear—whoever controlled the Nephilim controlled the end. But why did Ezekiel think that Michael or I would ever judge him to be "righteous and elect"? Ezekiel would be at the top of my list of sinners.

Ezekiel took center stage. With a flourish, he stretched out his hands in our direction and announced, "The answer lies in your name, Ellspeth."

What on earth did he mean?

He chuckled, as if I'd said my question aloud. I guessed that my face spoke volumes. "Ellspeth means the Chosen One. You are the Elect One."

"Me? Why not Michael?" The words just blurted out.

"Oh, Michael has a special role. But more in the nature of protector, a knight to his lady, if you will. Except you are so much more than a lady."

Stretching out his hand, he said, "Come with me."

So it was me. The Elect One. This was insane. And why did Ezekiel think I would go anywhere with him? Better than anyone, I knew his darkness; I had seen it firsthand through his own eyes.

I spun around and looked at Tamiel and Michael for

help. Michael's face still bore that glazed expression. And Tamiel hadn't left, but she had averted her eyes and stepped away from me and Michael and Ezekiel. Almost as if she was forbidden to join us in this battle.

Only Ezekiel met my gaze. "Ellspeth, you have a choice. You can come with me and save Michael. Or you can choose Tamiel and her kind, and I will destroy Michael."

So that's how Ezekiel thought he could get me to go with him. He believed that I would never, ever risk Michael's life. Even for a greater good.

And Ezekiel could be right. How could I choose to destroy Michael?

"You cannot have her!" Michael suddenly awoke with a scream.

Inexplicably, Ezekiel cast an amused look in Michael's direction. "I've heard those words before. I think Hananel and Daniel said them to me the day you were born, Ellspeth."

Michael lifted off the ground and flew at the surprised Ezekiel, who still stood on the stage. He landed on him with such force that Ezekiel fell off the stage with a crash, narrowly missing an exposed iron rod that supported the platform. But the rod must have grazed Ezekiel's face, as blood trickled down his cheek. It was unsettling to see the immortal Ezekiel bleed.

Ezekiel stood up, wiped away the blood with his finger,

and then licked it. "You would kill me instead, son?"

"Son? I'm no son of yours," Michael yelled.

"That is precisely who you are," Ezekiel answered calmly.

Michael then flew off the stage toward Ezekiel. This time, Ezekiel was ready. He propelled himself upward, into the rafters high in the ceiling of the hall. As Michael followed him, I started to lift off in pursuit. I couldn't let Michael fight Ezekiel alone.

Tamiel pulled me down to the ground. "Michael must combat Ezekiel unaided."

I struggled to free myself from her grasp, but she was incredibly strong. "Michael is trying to protect me from Ezekiel. I can't let him do that by himself. He needs me."

Tamiel took me by the shoulders and stared into my face. "Ellspeth, only the child can kill the parent. Let Michael fulfill his destiny, if he can."

"Ezekiel is really his father?" I was shocked, although it explained the link between them. I thought Ezekiel had been speaking metaphorically.

"Yes, he is. Only one with Ezekiel's blood in his veins can destroy him."

The news tore my attention from the battle raging overhead. "But I thought angels couldn't procreate?"

"They usually can't. But you and Michael are unique."

"So we really are Nephilim?"

"Yes."

"Where are our mothers? Our human mothers?" I felt a sudden, deep yearning for mine.

Tamiel stared at the floor. "Your birth mothers are no longer with us."

"They're dead?" I wanted to cry, but knew I couldn't. I had to keep my focus.

She nodded slowly, still not meeting my eye.

"What about my father? Where is he?"

A crash sounded out above us. Ezekiel had flung Michael into the metal scaffolding bolstering the ceiling, and I screamed despite myself. I twisted and turned, trying to get out of Tamiel's grip so I could help him.

"Stay here, or you will only complicate matters for Michael," she ordered.

Tamiel's hold was unbreakable, leaving me no choice but to stare at the war above us. Michael and Ezekiel dove up and over and around the massive rafters reinforcing the ceiling. Each took equal turns harming the other, and for a time, I felt heartened that Michael might actually win the battle. But then Ezekiel caught Michael by the foot and swung his head into a huge beam. Michael flew away, but I knew he was badly hurt. I could smell the blood flowing from his wounds, and I could sense him weakening.

Suddenly, I knew how I could help. Somehow I wrenched Tamiel's hands off my shoulders and raced to the side of the stage. I looked up. Michael and Ezekiel were hovering directly above me. It was my moment.

I forced a sob and cried out, "Ezekiel, stop. I can't watch you hurt Michael any longer. Stop. I'll go with you. But only if you deliver him to me—unharmed and flying of his own accord—right here."

"No, Ellie!" Michael yelled back.

"Yes, Michael." I pointedly looked down at the exposed iron rod, hoping desperately that Ezekiel didn't catch my meaning as well. "It is the only way."

"You have made the right choice, Ellspeth," Ezekiel called out.

Side by side, they began their descent. Ezekiel was careful not to touch Michael, but he didn't let him out of his sight either. I stood near—but not next to—the iron rod, and watched as they neared the floor. Just before they touched down, I stretched out my arms to Ezekiel, to distract him.

"It is almost time," I said. As if to Ezekiel.

Ezekiel reached out his arms for me. With an expression of triumph, he looked away from Michael and smiled at me. Just then, Michael flew at Ezekiel's back and shoved him into the iron rod with all his strength.

We raced to Ezekiel's side to make sure the deed was done. But we needn't have. Within seconds, the smell of the blood pouring from his body was overpowering. He seemed weak—even near death—but his eyes were still open and blinking.

"I am not alone. There are others. Others even more powerful than me. Like your father," Ezekiel whispered, and smiled his sick smile out at the crowd. And then the blinking stopped.

I looked out at Quincy Market, in the direction of Ezekiel's final gaze. There, in the throngs, I spotted a man with black hair and bright blue eyes staring right at us. As if he saw us. Then he disappeared.

Tamiel raced to our sides. She nodded in agreement with Ezekiel's last words. It was over, but only for the moment.

I didn't care. I stood up and hugged Michael as hard as I could. Even if we had only a short time of peacefulness together, even if I was this other, elect, strange creature, I wanted this moment, this moment of peace.

We looked into each other's eyes and smiled. I closed my eyes and surrendered into the warmth of Michael's arms.

FORTY-SEVEN

I opened my eyes. I was in my bedroom.

My bedroom.

I had no memory of returning to Tillinghast from Boston.

How had I gotten here? The last thing I remembered was holding on to Michael in Quincy Market, after we looked down at the body of Ezekiel. Oh my God, Ezekiel.

I sat up in my bed. I lifted up my quilt, blanket, and sheets. I was in my flannel pajamas. Who had dressed me in these? I looked at the clock. It said seven A.M., but I had no idea what day it was.

Pushing off my quilt, blanket, and sheets, I stood up, a little unsteady on my feet. I tottered over to my desk, where my bag sat. I picked it up, looking for any scrap of evidence that I'd been to Boston. I found my notebook filled with the usual scribbles, my wallet with my identification and money, and my toiletry bag stocked as always. There were no ticket stubs or receipts or even any of the lists of questions I'd made on the train to Boston or during that long night in the Harvard Square coffee shop. But my cell was there. The cell phone I'd thrown into the garbage can at the Tillinghast train station.

Had it all been a dream? The flying and the blood? Ezekiel and the trip to Boston? All that stuff about the Nephilim and the Elect One? Was Michael a dream too?

I ran downstairs, not sure what to hope for. My mom stood at the kitchen counter buttering toast and pouring orange juice, like she did every morning. She looked up at me, unsurprised that I stood in the kitchen. But she was surprised at my state, given the hour.

"Dearest, why are you still in your pajamas? You have to leave for school in five minutes."

I stared around the kitchen, as if I hadn't seen it in months. The kettle sat in its typical place, and the magnets on the fridge held up the normal pictures and reminders. Everything looked the same as when I left. But I felt entirely different.

My mom marched over to me and placed her hand on my forehead. "Do you feel sick, Ellie? You look a little peaked, but you don't feel warm."

I was afraid to speak. Almost any sentence that came out of my mouth could be really out of place. Even crazy.

"Dearest, is everything all right?"

Words finally croaked out of my mouth. "I'm okay, Mom. I just woke up from a really weird dream."

Her eyebrows rose in alarm, but her voice sounded calm. Very, very calm. "What was the dream, dearest?"

"Nothing. Just a dream. I'd better get ready."

I walked back upstairs and opened my closet to pick out an outfit. Hanging on the rack were some of the more daring clothes I'd bought since I started seeing Michael. And the red dress I'd worn to the Fall Dance. That wasn't a dream, at least. Maybe Michael wasn't either.

I grabbed a pair of jeans and a sweater and headed into the bathroom. Standing against the closed bathroom door for a long moment, I finally went over to the sink and turned on the hot water. As the steam rose up, I stared at myself in the foggy mirror. How could I look like the same old Ellie when so much had happened? Or had it?

But what choice did I have but to go through the motions of normalcy? I washed my face with my favorite lemony soap. I brushed out all the knots in my hair. I put on some blush and mascara, and I got dressed. All the while trying to ignore the sinking feeling in the pit of my stomach.

Dreading the uncertainty of school, I trudged back downstairs. "I'm ready to go, Mom."

She looked at me curiously. "But Michael's picking you up today."

"I'm not grounded anymore?" Michael hadn't been allowed to drive me to school since the Fall Dance. We were only allowed to see each other in supervised settings, like school or home.

"No, dearest. Your grounding was over this weekend." She paused and then asked, "Are you sure that you're all right, Ellie?"

"I'm fine, Mom." I hoped I sounded more convincing than I felt. I didn't want her to be worrying about me; I had enough troubles. "I'll just go wait by the front window for Michael."

"Do you want me to wait with you?"

"No thanks, Mom. I need to review my homework anyway." I needed a moment alone. And she seemed pleased that I mentioned something as normal as homework.

Staring out at the driveway, I tried to make sense of things. The list of questions that I'd written on the train to Boston kept coming back to me. If the past couple of months had been real—instead of some bizarre dream—then I might have a few answers to those questions.

What was I? The million-dollar question. Assuming the flying and the blood and Ezekiel and Boston had actually happened, I was pretty sure that I was a Nephilim. But aside from the powers it brought me, I wasn't certain what that meant. What was the purpose of a Nephilim? If I believed Ezekiel, then I was the "Elect One" with some special role in the "end days," whatever that entailed. Even my parents had said something about me being different and preparing for "war," and Tamiel had mentioned "end days." What was this war, and who would I be fighting against?

I still had more questions than answers. Like what had happened to my birth parents. Like whether I could count on Michael while I tried to figure this all out.

Just then, I heard the crunch of gravel. Michael's car pulled into our roundabout. My anxiety—already sky-high—mounted. What would I say to him? I still wasn't certain what was real and what was a dream.

"Bye, Mom," I called out, and walked to his car. The day was cool and drizzly, chilly but not cold enough for snow.

Michael turned off the ignition and opened the door for me from the inside. I slid in and closed it tightly behind me. Then I sat silently, uncertain what words were appropriate.

He reached over and kissed me on the cheek. "How was your night?"

"Fine," I answered warily. "Yours?"

"Good. I finished that awful calculus assignment," he said as he turned the key in the ignition.

"That's great." I didn't know what to say next. I couldn't even remember what homework I'd been working on before I fled to Boston. So I stayed quiet.

The car started, and music flooded the car. The song was Coldplay, "Cemeteries of London." It was one of my favorites, as Michael knew. It reminded me of our night-time flying and exploring. If those things really happened, that was.

"Feels like London out today, doesn't it?" Michael said.

I looked over at him in surprise. Had he just said what I thought he had? We had been heading to London to see Professor Barr the day before—from Boston. Or was he just referring to the song?

A smile spread across his face. A knowing smile.

"So . . . ?" My mind raced. It hadn't been a dream.

As if reading my thoughts, Michael said, "Ignorance is the only thing that has protected you so far."

In that instant, I realized what had happened. In the con-versation among our parents that Michael had overheard, my dad had said the same thing. Our parents wanted so badly to keep us in the dark about our identities—for our protection and to prevent the ticking of the end days clock—that they'd attempted to have our memories erased. About flying and Ezekiel and Boston and the Nephilim and the Elect One. They knew better than to try to make us forget each other; they had tried it after Guatemala, and it hadn't fully worked.

It had failed again here. We remembered everything.

I started to talk excitedly. All the pieces were falling into place. But Michael shook his head and put a finger over my lips.

So I just smiled back at Michael. I knew that this wasn't the end. It was only the beginning.

Turn the page for an exclusive excerpt of

The captivating sequel to *Fallen Angel*!

Stepping into the hallways of Tillinghast High School was actually weirder than acknowledging that I was an otherworldly creature.

I watched as girls chatted about their lip gloss, and guys shared apps on their iPhones. I noticed friends giggling about other friends' outfits, and teammates thumping each other on the backs for games well-played. I walked past kids furiously copying their friends' homework assignments, and others fumbling with the towers of books in their lockers.

I couldn't stop from staring at my classmates in amazement, like they were exotic creatures in the zoo. They had no idea that some kind of Armageddon was heading their way and that I was selected to play some special role at the end. Maybe even stop it.

I felt the simultaneous urge to sob and giggle. Because the whole notion of Ellspeth Faneuil as savior to the world was both overwhelming and ridiculous.

The only thing keeping me sane while I walked down the hallway was Michael. The link of his fingers in mine was like a tether to our new reality. I believed I could navigate through our conflicting worlds—the frivolous Tillinghast

High School and the looming otherworldly battle—with him beside me.

But once I said good-bye to Michael before heading into English class, I lost my anchor. I felt like I'd been cast unmoored into an unreal sea.

English class brought me near to the brink. The minute I entered the classroom, Miss Taunton launched into me. Like a hawk circling a wounded animal, she bombarded me with questions about our latest assigned novel, which I could barely remember amid the more vivid recollections of my days in Boston and my encounter with Ezekiel. I wanted to scream at her that none of this mattered.

The second that Miss Taunton laid off me, my best friend, Ruth, texted me. "Wait for me in the hall after class." Normally, I'd welcome a quick chat with my oldest and best friend in the world, especially if it involved commiseration over Miss Taunton's unfair, but not unusual, treatment of me. But I didn't know if I could handle a one-on-one conversation with Ruth just yet. I had no idea what she remembered. The last time we were together—just before I boarded the train to Boston—she had confessed to seeing me fly. Had my parents tried to erase Ruth's memory, too, with more success? If so, could I pull off the act of regular Ellie? I pled illness and intermittently coughed throughout class to support my ruse.

At the ringing of the bell, I raced out of class. My head

was spinning. I needed a moment to catch my breath, to reassemble myself.

Instead, I ran smack into Piper. My next-door neighbor and one of the most popular girls in school had been ignoring me for weeks since I decided to take the blame for that wicked Facebook prank. Unbelievably, she had decided that this was the moment to break the silence.

"I know what you did, Ellie. I just don't get why you did it. Why would you take the blame for something you didn't do? Why would you sit through weeks of detention and walk down the hallways knowing that all the kids in school hate you? Without ever pointing the finger at me or Missy. I bet you think you're some kind of a saint," she said with a flip of her perfect blond hair.

I didn't know what to say. Part of me wanted to tell her the truth. That her snide little guess wasn't totally off the mark. I was a half-angel, and I simply couldn't have sat by and let others suffer at her hand. That she better rethink her future actions and ask forgiveness for those past, because there wasn't much time left for malevolent games.

The conversation nearly delivered me to the edge. Who was I meant to be? How was I supposed to behave, knowing what I knew?

Before I said anything I'd regret, Michael appeared at my side.

He had been waiting for me after class, farther down the hall. When he saw Piper accost me and witnessed my obvious discomfort at the exchange, he raced to my rescue.

"Are you all right, Ellie? You look really pale," he asked, once we were alone. I must have looked really bad, because alarm registered on his face.

"I'm not sure if I can do this, Michael. I know we need to pretend, but I'm having a hard time already. Knowing what we know," I whispered.

Michael put his arm around my shoulder and walked me down the hallway. He brought us into a darkened alcove. More than anything, I wanted to stay in that warm, shadowy recess, wrapped in his arms. It was the only place I felt safe. It was the only place that made sense.

Michael placed his finger under my chin, and tipped my face to his. "Ellie, I know you can." He slipped a letter into my hands. He nodded that I should read it immediately, so I smoothed out the paper and started.

My Ellie —

Do you remember the first time we went flying over our field? You were so nervous of everything. You were afraid to fall from such heights; you didn't want to embarrass yourself in front of me; you were fearful of doing something so clearly otherworldly. But you were determined and strong. And I watched in awe as you furrowed your beautiful brow, willed your fears away, and took to the air.

You were breathtaking up there. The wind at your back, your black hair whipping all around you—you owned the skies. From the very beginning.

And the very next day, you walked down the hallways of Tillinghast High School like nothing had happened. Like you were just a regular girl—prettier and smarter than all the rest, of course, but still just a regular, human girl.

You can do that again, Ellie. You can walk the tightrope between the two worlds with courage and determination. You've done it before.

I love you,
Michael

I smiled as I read the letter. Somehow he had anticipated my feelings, and understood—perfectly—how to restore my confidence. How to bring me back to myself. Michael truly was my soul mate.

"Thank you," I whispered.

"Just remember who you are. Remember that you walked this walk before, and you can do it again."

I nodded and closed my eyes for a second. Conjuring those days from earlier in the fall, my self-assurance returned. Slowly and shakily. I really had no other option. I *had* to successfully playact at being a regular high school junior, concerned about homework and her new boyfriend. Michael *had* to convincingly make-believe that he was an average senior guy, focused on football and college prospects and me. Too much depended on our role-playing.

Feeling fairly confident, off to calculus I went. As I listened to Mr. Modic rattle off theorems, I stopped fixating on the surreal nature of my situation and started to map out next steps. By the time class ended, and I joined Michael in the hallway, I wasn't surprised that his next letter had the same focus. I had already drafted a similar note in my head.

> *My Ellie—*
>
> *Now that your resolve has returned, did you spend all of calculus thinking about what we should do next? I know you well. I bet you didn't take a single note, but instead stared out the window, dreaming up a strategy.*
>
> *I did the same thing.*
>
> *What should we do next? The trip to Boston definitely gave us a better sense of our natures as Nephilim, and the encounter with Ezekiel linked our*

births to the emergence of some kind of apocalypse. Crazy as that sounds. But we need much more information in order to act next. We need to know exactly what the Nephilim are and were—creation, history, powers, even mortality— and we need to know how the Nephilim fit into this whole end-of-the-world scenario that Ezekiel revealed to us.

But how are we going to get that knowledge—about ourselves and the end days—while playing dumb and suppressing our powers? Wouldn't any research we undertook—either in a library or on the ground—serve as a red flag to our parents or anyone else who might be seeking us? We need to act, but what do we do?

My brilliant, brilliant Ellie. Did you drum up any amazing ideas in calculus? We need a plan. Now.

I love you,
Michael

Between the last few periods of the day, we exchanged a flurry of letters. We each had our theories on how best to get the information we required, and they weren't the same.

Finally, by the end of the school day, we concocted a

plan we could both agree upon. It was risky. But really, it was our only choice.

★   ★   ★

When the last bell rang, I walked Michael over to the football field for his practice, just as I would any other day. We had decided to keep as close as possible to our usual activities and schedule. Just in case.

Before he headed into the locker room, I leaned in to kiss him, as I always did. But today, instead of the usual "see you later," I heard him whisper, "good luck."

I needed it.

I walked over to the parking lot to meet Ruth for an after-school coffee, having texted her that my cough had subsided and I felt up to our regular meeting. It sickened me to lie to her; we'd always told each other everything.

Amid all the cars and all the kids preparing to bolt from school, I didn't spot her at first. But then I caught a glint of her red hair against the backdrop of the gray day. I hustled over to her used, green VW Bug, not sure what reaction I'd get. Did she remember seeing me fly or didn't she? How was I supposed to behave?

"You look *really* ready for a latte," Ruth pronounced, sounding very normal.

"I am *really* ready for one," I said, attempting to match her light tone.

As we got into her car, I thought how pretty she looked under those wire-rimmed glasses. I smiled a little thinking about how shocked our classmates had been when Ruth unleashed her inner runway model at the fall dance. Only to tuck that beauty away again for school on Monday. Loyal, whip-smart, but incredibly reserved, Ruth loathed any unnecessary attention. She saved up her animation and lovely smiles for a select few, and most of Tillinghast High School didn't make that cut. I just hoped that the frank conversation I planned for our coffee break wouldn't wipe the pretty grin right off her face.

I tried to mask my nervousness as we rode to the Daily Grind, and to bolster my courage by remembering the words of Michael's first letter that day. We chatted away, mostly about a benign argument she had had with her new boyfriend, Jamie, about his chronic lateness. The conversation continued as we ordered our coffees and settled into two brown club chairs that sat side by side. As I feigned interest, I lifted my latte to my mouth for a sip. Suddenly, I noticed that my hand was shaking. I put the cup down on the table; I didn't want Ruth to see and wonder why. Not quite yet, anyway.

Once she finished, I waited until the Daily Grind buzzed with noise. Then I scanned the room to make sure no one was paying us the slightest attention. Leaning over the arm of my chair, I slipped a piece of paper into her lap.

I prayed that the information divulged within wouldn't shatter her world. More fervently, I prayed that, after she read the contents of the letter, she wouldn't decide Michael and I were crazy and alert my parents to the disclosure—in an effort to "help" us with our delusions, of course. That would undermine everything that Michael and I were trying to accomplish.

Either way, it was a gamble Michael and I had to take. We had no other options.

Ruth stared down at the letter sitting in her lap, and said, "What's this?"

"Just read it, Ruth. Please."

Laughing, she said, "So we're passing notes now? What are we, in the third grade?"

I bit my lip and motioned for her to read the letter that Michael and I had so painstakingly crafted. Hesitantly, she picked it up and unfolded it. I held my breath as she did. In the letter, we told her everything we knew. We begged her to help us better understand who we were and what the end days were. We couldn't undertake the research ourselves; if anyone was looking for us or watching us, they would realize that we *knew*.

Even though Ruth had been my best friend for nearly

ten years, I really didn't know how she would respond to our plea for help researching the nature of the Nephilim and the looming apocalypse. How could I possibly predict her reaction to the claim that I was an angel of some sort? That our world teetered on the edge of annihilation?

Ruth cleared her throat, and whispered, "So you *do* remember?"

I was flabbergasted. Nothing in her behavior had given me the slightest hint that she remembered anything. "You do too?"

Ruth leaned toward me. In a voice so low that I could barely hear it, she said, "I remember watching you and Michael fly. And I remember taking you to the train station a few days ago. Today is the first day I've seen you since. I've been so worried about you and Michael, but who could I ask? Certainly not your parents."

Relief coursed through me. I reached over to hug her, and said, "Thank God."

Ruth squeezed me back, and whispered, "I thought you had forgotten what you could do, or that I knew about your and Michael's . . . abilities. Or that you didn't want to talk about it for some reason. So when you pretended you were sick earlier today, I kind of backed away from you."

"Now you know why I haven't mentioned it." I tried to apologize. I felt her nod against my shoulder.

"So you'll help us?" I whispered.

"Yes, Ellie. I'll do the research that you and Michael need."

"You understand that there are risks? Huge risks?"

"Of course. That seems very clear." Even though her voice sounded firm and strong, I wondered if she really comprehended the dangers. How could she, unless she'd stared evil in the face as Michael and I had?

I started to cry. "Thank you, Ruth. Thank you so much for helping me and Michael."

"Ellie, I'd do anything for you. You know that. But, I'm not just doing this for you and Michael."

"No?"

"I am doing this for everyone, Ellie. Because if I understand your letter correctly, everyone is at risk. And the entire world is at stake."